Tidal Pulse: Mars Revolution

Fusion in a Fission World, Volume 2

S.V. Farnsworth

Published by Stone Wolfe Press, 2024.

This is a work of fiction. Similarities to real people, places, or events are entirely coincidental.

TIDAL PULSE: MARS REVOLUTION

First edition. October 10, 2024.

Copyright © 2024 S.V. Farnsworth.

ISBN: 978-1961221000

Written by S.V. Farnsworth.

Also by S.V. Farnsworth

Fusion in a Fission World
Hard Start: Mars Intrigue
Tidal Pulse: Mars Revolution

Modutan Empire
Woman of the Stone
Monarch in the Flames

Standalone
A Rare Connection: Inspirational Romantic Suspense
Tucked Away in a Discolored Scrapbook: Creative Nonfiction with
Poetry

Watch for more at https://svfarnsworthauthor.com.

Table of Contents

With thanks to God, my family, and my friends.

Chapter One

Royce Nedge hunted predators from the center of the sunny promenade of Mars Colony NINE. Concealed behind the tinted visor of a shock suit, he flexed his muscular arms and folded them across his broad chest. Passers-by took notice and avoided him.

His zeal as an executioner was that of an avenging angel. Alik had trained him well, but his mentor's death a month ago had wounded Royce deeply. In truth, his faith in a merciful God had been shaken to the core when he'd discovered it was due to Lisa Shim's betrayal of the trust he'd placed in her unwavering allegiance to the cause of freedom.

She had been his guiding star. Without her integrity intact, he'd resorted to seeking vengeance. Bent on pursuing a list of evil-doers living in NINE, he'd irrevocably compromised his iron-clad principles.

Not that he wanted to be bought and sold on the underground market for sex, but food cost credits, and infant formula was rationed. His empty stomach rumbled at the aroma from a nearby vendor's grill with no way to satisfy it.

Standing amidst the tall pine trees of NINE, he fully understood the dangers he faced and the consequences of his actions. His mother had wisely forbidden him to come. Yet, when he'd failed to find the man most responsible for his suffering, he'd taken the risk.

The incompetent Technology Director that Lisa was replacing, huffed and puffed as he walked along the promenade toward the docking ring. Five underlings carried bags and rolled trunks in a formation behind him. Xyler's much younger wife trailed the throng wearing a glitzy outfit and precariously high heels.

Royce had waited for this sign. The elite class was fleeing NINE for the Incursion Zone. He headed for the nearest stairwell, descending the steps three at a time on his way to sub-level one's communications center.

He strode in as if he belonged there and sat at a console, tuning the shortwave radio's frequency. Men and women bustled about, monitoring private citizens' communications. A pair of men entered the large room, one had his arm around the shoulder of the other as they watched a data pad with animated expressions.

"He's huge." One man pointed.

"She's not, but in he goes." The other man laughed.

"Replay it again at half speed." The second man leaned closer to the screen.

Royce stood as they walked past to see the infrared recording of a man and a woman coupling. None of this spying on citizens was legal. Yet, that didn't seem to bother the Space Division personnel involved.

Royce clenched his gloved hand around the microphone, sitting at the radio instead of confronting the voyeurs. "The guests are on their way. Over."

The radio belched static for a moment. "We're dressed for the party. Over and out."

Royce changed the frequency to obscure his activity and left the communications center, heading for the docking ring. He double-timed it up the stairs to a long, curved, hallway of windows and hatches. Rovers of various sizes backed up to take on passengers.

Black uniformed Police Division officers maintained order despite the massive crowd. Space Division pilots in silver-gray uniforms boarded the people on their manifests into rovers. The pompous Xyler and his shrill entourage argued about being left behind as armed police ushered them from the ring.

A vindictive thrill coursed along Royce's spine. Xyler's devious plotting hadn't resulted in the hoped for reward. He'd never enter the Incursion Zone or receive the promised luxuries.

Other elites, however, fled from NINE in droves, departing in all types of rovers amidst the stunning, red rock landscape. Their pilots accelerated the land crafts north along the spur and entered the equatorial Glass Highway, heading East. He wished them a fiery death on the road tonight.

Would Lisa stay or travel with the group? Surely, the Matchmaker would go. Royce's blood warmed for the kill.

Unexpectedly, his gaze struck a familiar blonde woman. Her golden blouse with trim-fitting slacks of a similar shade, marked her as a high ranking member of the Administrative Division. He froze in place among the crowd, moved by the vulnerability in her nervous turning of a narrow, wedding band on her left hand.

Fortunately for him, no one questioned an undercover Space Division agent while in full shock gear no matter how in the way he might be. His mother had aged gracefully. From the moment she'd discovered him in the dungeon of Laser Outpost Indigo in his early childhood, she'd shielded him from most of the abuse that illegally held slaves suffered.

Standing at hatch thirty-nine, she chewed her bottom lip until the coral colored lipstick wore away. Eleven months ago, she'd finally found a way to free him from captivity. She'd sent Alik to break him out, take him into the Northern Territory, and provide military training.

Looking at her now, the depth of his gratitude stirred to life once more inside his chest. The debt he owed her could never be repaid, but freeing slaves in her service had given him hope. Consumed by his descent into despair, he'd dealt in nothing but death of late, and he knew she'd disapprove.

Any contact with her would put them both at risk, but he couldn't let her board a rover. Not when the revolutionaries had laid a trap on the highway tonight. So, he strode forward and took her right hand as if to shake it.

"Delay your departure." He stroked a birthmark on her thumb the way she had caressed his matching one when she'd identified him in the slave lineup so long ago. "It isn't safe."

She raised the ring on her left hand behind her right ear. Wincing in pain, she nearly collapsed. Royce steadied her, but she urged him to move along the wall of windows.

Understanding her caution, he strode to the next hatch and stood at attention. She braced a hand on the glass, hunched over in seeming distress. He watched her out of the corner of his eye.

"Son, you're wrong about Lisa." A pleading look filled her agonized gaze. "She wasn't to blame for Alik's death. Shade was nervous and tried to boost the range of the roadside electromagnetic pulse device. You know how she fiddled with everything. Well, it broke. So, Alik rolled a rock onto the Glass Highway. He was hit and Shade was crushed in the rover accident."

"I don't believe you." He stiffened. "Why are you telling me this?"

"Because–" She groaned still holding the ring behind her ear. "Cody Greene is also my son. The enemy will bring him and his wife here soon. Please, help me defeat the Matchmaker and escape with us."

"Cody is my brother?" Royce stood taller, staring straight ahead. "Why didn't you tell me?"

"I should have told you both." Her hand dropped from behind her ear.

The shuffling steps from his tortured past sounded from the opposite direction. A white haired man held onto the rail of a patient occupied hospital gurney while the red uniformed Health Division Director Andrea Tran pushed it along the hallway. The old man's smug expression caused heinous acts of remembered violation to ripple across Royce's skin and his rapid breathing to rebound inside his helmet.

Two massive, armed guards flanked either side of the gurney. Outwardly stolid, Royce stood straight with his heart palpitating, immobilized by visions from the past as the Matchmaker passed him. Cody lay unconscious in a hospital gown on the gurney. What had they done to him?

"Father." Royce's mother addressed the Matchmaker. "Why isn't Lisa with you?"

"I'll take care of her, Addison." The elderly villain grasped Royce's mother's arm, drawing her away from the hatch to allow Director Tran to wheel Cody inside. "I know where she's gone." He ruled a criminal empire in obscurity, wearing the blue uniform of a lowly Technology Division programmer to hide in plain sight.

"Let her finish her task." Addison shied away from her father's touch. "It might help the situation."

"No." The Matchmaker's thin lips pressed together. "Lisa is wasting her time repairing the fifth atmospheric collector. It won't be enough to save the colony from environmental collapse. You should take Cody to Laser Outpost Juliet. I'll meet you there."

"You must not hurt her." Addison's facial features sagged in a pitiable way as if she might weep. "My son will never forgive me if you do."

"Act fast." The Matchmaker smiled with a glint in his eyes. "The doctor has implanted the stimulation device, but Cody will wake up from the sedative soon. Have her perform the match the instant you depart unless you want my grandson to know what you've agreed to in exchange for leniency."

"I'll keep my word." Color rose in Addison's cheeks. "Is the doctor's husband safely at Juliet?"

"Not yet." The Matchmaker's gaze narrowed. "He's driving a wrecker as part of the escort for a convoy of elites in case anything goes wrong. Let's meet there in the morning. I want to see their faces when you tell them what you've arranged. Anyway, I'll bring Lisa shortly. You go ahead and leave without me."

"Yes, Father." Addison's chin dropped in a defeated pose.

The old man smiled as he shuffled along the emptying hallway carrying a medical kit. One of the guards protected him. The second man pointed his rifle at Addison.

Royce watched his mother stare as the Matchmaker moved away. The trembling of her hands was visible even from a distance. Had the Matchmaker abused her too?

The ease with which he had molested Royce and ordered his other grandson's exploitation solidified the impression. Pain showed in his mother's mournful eyes. She inhaled a tremulous breath, facing the open hatch of the waiting transport with the corners of her lips turned downward.

"Please, end our suffering. I love you, my son." She entered the hatch.

The guard entered with her, sealing them inside. Without delay, the craft departed into the fading light of an orange sunset. Why hadn't he done anything?

Dread for his mother and brother's well being assailed him, but he steadied his nerves by fixating on Addison's vengeful command. He would take pleasure in murdering the Matchmaker. The man deserved it for the suffering he'd inflicted.But Royce could not spare Lisa Shim, not even for his brother's sake. No, she had destroyed his hope for redemption when she'd joined the enemy's service. And for that unfaithful act of treachery, she must pay the ultimate price.

Chapter Two

Determined to deliver retribution, Royce strode toward bio-dome number five. Far ahead of him on the promenade, his depraved grandfather and his guard entered the service elevator, ascending to the third floor. After two minutes, Royce did the same, drawing a throwing knife from his belt.

The doors opened onto a balcony above the ocean habitat. The matchmaker's guard spun around, bringing his pulse rifle to bear. But before he fired a shot, Royce's blade sunk into the man's throat.

The man stumbled forward, falling dead part way into the elevator car. The surf pounded on the sand below. Heart thudding in his ears, Royce stepped over the body, inhaling the humid air that carried the scents of salt and sea creatures even through the filters of his shock suit's helmet.

The sheer size of the bio-dome dwarfed him to insignificance. Daunted by the height of the open space, he forced one boot forward and then the other. He'd lived much of his life confined to a two by three meter mating suite.

Now, a vast body of water stretched before him. The view of the waves from up here made him dizzy. Ahead of him lay a narrow catwalk.

The Matchmaker made his way toward the other end. The crash of the surf obscured his footfalls. Royce crouched level with the railing and started across the catwalk in pursuit.

From the platform at the far end of the bio-dome, Lisa's feminine voice raised in protest. Royce couldn't make out the words. However, her distress gave him grim satisfaction.

Lisa's two burly bodyguards seized her arms. As she struggled, the Matchmaker slapped her hard across the face. Then, the guards slammed her to the deck plating.

Confused, Royce crept closer. At the Matchmaker's command, the guards stripped Lisa's environmental suit from her body. Then, they spread her legs.

"I've never operated a speculum before." The Matchmaker withdrew something from the medical kit. "But I think this is how it works."

The vicious man inserted the device into Lisa's most intimate place. Yet, she didn't make a sound. Nor did she fight, though she had argued before.

The Matchmaker thrust a long cotton swab into her body, removed it, then sealed it in a tube, placing the sample in his pocket. Only breeding stock were treated this way. Was Lisa in the program?

Rage swelled in Royce's chest until a killing frenzy overcame his fear of death. He drew a serrated knife from the sheathe strapped to his thigh. Launching an attack on the guards, he plunged the blade into the nearest man's side.

The other guard blasted him in the chest with an up swinging stun rifle. Royce's shock suit absorbed the pulse, crackling with the electrical charge. He stabbed the henchman in the heart.

The Matchmaker fled, but Royce tripped him. The gut-stabbed guard stood, slamming the butt of his rifle into Royce's helmet. Trampling Lisa underfoot, Royce slashed at the man's neck.

Amidst a spray of blood, the guard toppled. The bio-dome resounded with a solid thud as his lifeless body hit the deck. Royce caught his breath, spotting the Matchmaker partway across the catwalk.

Facing the woman he'd intended to torture, Royce studied her naked, unmoving body. Her eyes stared, unblinking. Did she retreat into herself the way he did when bad things happened?

No, that couldn't be right because her eyes focused on him. Yet, she lay prone in the most humiliating way. Why didn't she react?

He turned his boot to shove the speculum deeper. Surely that was painful, but she made no sound. Had the guards paralyzed her when they'd slammed her to the deck?

He crouched, removed the metal speculum, and stared at her bleeding body from behind the visor of his helmet. She was torn in several places. Her purity had been real.

He ground his teeth. Inexplicably incensed, he stood and threw the speculum at her. It hit her in the ribs, causing a small gash in her flesh to drip blood.

Unflinching of body, this time her eyelids twitched. Dark-rimmed glasses framed her expressive blue eyes and tears wetted the sides of her face. None of this made sense.

"I came here to kill you." He removed his gloves and helmet. "You may not remember, but I choked the life out of you three weeks ago. I had planned to rip you to pieces, but I see someone has already done that for me."

Her silence and incessant tears added to his uneasiness. A droplet of blood on her neck looked different. That single drop stood out amidst the arterial spray that had misted her body.

He glanced into the medical kit to find a half-drained syringe. The Matchmaker had injected her with a paralytic. Her labored breathing elicited pity, but Royce scoffed at his stupid sympathies.

"A virgin." He shook his head. "I'd heard rumors, but I never believed that a director could be virtuous." Scowling, he met her gaze. "That's too bad."

The Matchmaker's limping gait reverberated on the catwalk grating. With an injured knee, his progress was slow. Royce picked up the speculum and grabbed a handful of swabs, making plans to extract information from the tyrant.

Royce's solid footfalls shook the catwalk. Panting, the crippled man pulled along the railing to hurry his faltering steps. Royce savored the sport of the hunt.

"I'm not here to recapture you." The Matchmaker gasped for breath, without looking back. "Your replacement is on his way to Outpost Juliet. If you leave now, then there will be no reprisal."

Royce shoved the fiend forward onto his face. "The punishments awaiting you are long overdue." He dragged the Matchmaker's pants down past his knees.

"Please, don't hurt me." The reprobate trembled violently. "I was only doing my job. I'll give you anything you want."

"Pain is inevitable in life." Royce had pleaded for mercy as a child but received none. "It's your turn."

He thrust the speculum into the Matchmaker's backside without regard for his screams of distress. Widening the device to the maximum, Royce thrust the swabs into the opening as far as they would go. His thirst for vengeance remained unsated.

"When did Lisa Shim join the Gold Circle?" Royce had to know the answer.

"She isn't confederate." Convulsing, the elderly man flailed as if bewildered. "She isn't even an elite anymore. That opportunity has passed. She'll never see the outside of a dungeon again."

"Why?" Royce slammed the speculum in deeper.

The Matchmaker's eyes rolled back in his head for four heartbeats, but then he came around. "She resists our orders. She won't take the oath. We can't allow her to remain free. That's why I'm taking her to Juliet."

"I don't believe you." Royce had been deceived before by this man. "How long ago did Lisa Shim betray her people and her religion for money?"

"Her philosophy cares nothing for wealth." The Matchmaker's teeth set on edge. "She has betrayed the greater good by disobeying me." He adjusted his position to meet Royce's gaze. "Fortunately for her, I require her to reproduce. My grandson bred her today. She'll mother my successor. I'll make sure of it myself if Cody won't." He grinned. "She can supply a dozen offspring over time. There's no reason you and I can't share in creating them." His brows drew together. "You may have her next, just let me live."

"You would give the great Lisa Shim to me?" Royce's fists shook.

"I'll ask for her return at some point." The Matchmaker craned his neck to make eye contact. "But you may delight in her until then."

"I came here to execute her for corruption, not to become a part of it." Royce sensed duplicity in the old man. "You speak nothing but lies."

"I'm giving you what I planned to take." The devious man's jaw set. "It's a generous offer. Let's keep her in the family."

"Family?" Royce convulsed in a violent wave of revulsion. "I want nothing from you but as much restitution as I can carve from your flesh."

"You have no right to restitution." The Matchmaker's expression twisted. "I replicated you in secret to take Cody's place in the breeding program because his mother wouldn't let me have him, but now he's mine and you're free. Let me live and I will continue to conceal your illicit existence."

"I'm Cody Greene's clone?" Royce struggled for breath.

"Yes." The Matchmaker strained to rise from the grating. "That's why the matchmaking software pared you with so many women." He chuckled. "Genetically speaking, you're nearly perfect."

"I don't look like him." Grinding his teeth, Royce flipped the man over and pressed a knee in the middle of his chest for a straight answer.

"Yes, you do." The Matchmaker grimaced with glassy eyes. "But you're right. You're better looking than my grandson. I enhanced your looks on a purely cosmetic level." He leered at Royce. "You've fulfilled my every fantasy."

Silenced by traumatic memories of past abuse, Royce used his knife to sever the sadistic man's reproductive motivation. Screaming in agony, the evil man thrashed Royce's chest with his fists. Undeterred, Royce cast each part into the waves below.

"Spare my life." The emasculated man lay pale and panting on the catwalk. "I'm begging you."

"While in NINE, I acquired something." Royce stabbed the point of his knife into the meat of his hand until his blood dripped into the Matchmaker's wounds. "Let's keep it between us."

"What are you doing?" The vile man's chest heaved with distress.

"I have the Rot." Royce raised up to plunge his knife into the man's heart.

"Rotcargathogen?" The Matchmaker rolled under the railing.

Shrieking, he fell into the ocean below. Flailing to the surface, he bobbed amidst the waves. Royce stood and slammed the railing with his hands in frustration.

Against all odds, the maimed monster swam for the shore. Regardless of what he'd said about giving Lisa away, he would doubtless alert the authorities. That put Royce in a bind for time.

He stalked along the catwalk toward the genius engineer who had designed the protocol to quietly transfer resources from one colony to another. There was no disputing that Lisa Shim's source code had placed the colonists in jeopardy. However, if she wasn't profiting from it, then who was?

A new list of suspects formed in his mind. Lisa's mother had the skills required, but considering her selfless, conservative leanings and her tender hearted ways, she seemed an unlikely thief. On the other hand, Lisa's sister, Sahra, harbored ambitions and had ample opportunity to steal a copy of the protocol.

His heart sank like a rock descending to the bottom of the ocean. He had made a catastrophic miscalculation. He'd pursued the wrong Shim.

Lisa lay before him helpless and broken. As a wordless confession of his shameful guilt, he stripped the silver, shock suit from his body. Wide eyed, Lisa stared at the three, little sores oozing on his hairless groin.

"Torturing you is all I've thought about since I found out Alik had died while intercepting your rover." He held her gaze. "I was sure you were to blame."

He reached into the medical kit, retrieved a tube of ointment, and spread the medicine on the diseased skin. Relief overpowered him. He closed his eyes and tilted his head back as his heavy breathing steadied.

Lisa's lack of a response belied the animation in her gaze. Paralyzed by the drug, she could not yet speak. However, her ability to blink had returned and her eyes tracked his movements.

He sensed recognition in her gaze. She'd known him as an intern named Praetorius and saved his life in a smoke filled water treatment facility. He'd repaid her valor with a murder attempt, because he hadn't believed a little thing like her could have dragged him to safety.

Royce knelt between her legs and took her cool, calloused hand in his. The feel of it surprised him since it testified of how hard she worked and witnessed of her strength. Smearing ointment on her fingers, he dragged her hand across her wounds in the hopes of easing her pain.

"The virgin director." He adjusted his gaze from the destruction Cody had wrought between her legs toward the perfect symmetry of her small breasts. "Until today, you were chaste. That corroborates the Matchmaker's confession. You are a slave, not a killer. I was wrong."

He stood and strode to the storage lockers, grabbing an environmental suit. "You'll come out of the paralytic in half an hour. Unfortunately, that randy, old goat will alert security in about eight minutes. I knew I should have cut out his liver. It was too much to ask that he'd drown."

She blinked, and in her eyes he saw that he had become the monster he'd been hunting. He scrunched the environmental suit, stepped into the boots, pulled the tight fitting covering over his musculature, and worked his broad shoulders through the neck hole. Only Lisa had the capacity to redeem him from damnation, and with death looming up to receive him, he needed her prayers more than ever.

"If I want answers from you, then I'll have to take you with me." He clenched his jaw. "At least this way, the Matchmaker will be denied his prize."

Royce grabbed her suit and forced her body into it. He ripped the communications devices out of their helmets and sealed Lisa up. In need of resources, he looted items of value from the guards' belts and pockets.

Cramming everything into Lisa's specialized toolkit, he attached the kit to a stun rifle's strap. He then removed his cursed, rectangular locket from around his neck and dropped it in the medical kit before attaching the kit to the second rifle's strap. In a crisscross pattern, he slung the rifles across his back.

Everything he took would come in handy in the barrens of the Northern Territories. But nothing was more valuable than Lisa. He secured his helmet and tossed her trim body over his shoulder, exiting through the airlock to cross the deadly, Martian desert at night.

Chapter Three

Lisa Shim-Greene gasped the shallow breaths of a dying woman. Slung over Mr. Praetorius' shoulder, her environmental suit offered limited protection against the intense, nighttime chill that sapped the heat from her body. Her fallen eyeglasses scratched back and forth inside her helmet with the relentless gate of the assassin who had almost succeeded in killing her once and doubtless planned to try again.

Her vision of Colony NINE's distant lights narrowed as her breathing rate increased. Mr. Praetorius had put her in the same suit she'd walked outside the bio-dome in when she fixed the atmospheric collector for the ocean habitat. Most likely, he hadn't realized she'd expended the bulk of the oxygen supply.

Everyone living in the colonies would die gasping if she didn't stop the Gold Council from siphoning away air. With her last cohesive thought, she prayed that God would spare her life. Gradually a warm feeling blossomed in her chest, bringing the impression that Cody needed her to live.

Mr. Praetorius hiked a steep incline, carrying Lisa toward what she hoped was adequate shelter. The temperature continued to drop to perilous levels, but she focused on slowing her breathing rate to conserve oxygen. When had she stopped shivering?

Something gave way beneath Mr. Praetorius' feet. He stepped upward, then settled her partially paralyzed body into a fully reclined seat. Behind her head, he secured everything he'd stolen.

The red indicator light blinking on her chest reflected off of his helmet. Blink. Blink.

His body startled, then he dropped to one knee beside her, plugging a life support hose into her suit. He sat her up straighter, squeezed in beside her on the seat, and plugged a second line into his suit. With the press of a button, warm, oxygen rich air circulated into her helmet.

"Everything all right over there?" He shook her shoulder.

His deep, hoarse voice sounded genuinely concerned. She managed a mumble in reply. Her head cleared slowly until her blinding headache eased.

He started the panels lifting from the ground to enfold the stealth rover's occupants. As soon as they were concealed, he piloted the craft using the right handed control panel. The ripple-tracks would leave no trace of their passing across the sands of Mars.

"The drug should have worn off by now." He wrapped an arm around her, and pulled her close to his side.

The added warmth of his body raised her temperature enough to rescue her from hypothermia. Soon she shivered in a healthy response to the cold. After another ten minutes, the feeling in her fingers returned.

"Thank you." Her gratitude for his saving her from the Matchmaker and his henchmen overpowered her resentment for a moment. "Why rescue me?"

"You're a slave." He tucked her hand under his arm. "And you know how my husband died."

"Who was your husband?" Lisa shivered violently.

"His name was Alik. He and my friends intercepted your rover last month." Praetorius' voice grated darkly.

"Oh." She tried to control her shaking body, but that made it worse. "I'll tell you as much about that day as I can. Cody and I married that morning in SEVEN, and we stopped in EIGHT for half an hour so I could see the colony."

"I spotted you at the docking ring." Praetorius pulled her closer. "I was watching for you and radioed Alik about your movements."

"You did?" She had noticed a towering man in a shock suit that day. "Well, that explains how the outlaws knew I was traveling. Anyway, that night between EIGHT and Indigo, our rover smashed into something in the road. We rolled until we collided with a boulder." Tammy, the secretary to Gold Council Member Addison Albright, had ordered her not to say anything more. "That's all I can say. Please, take me back to NINE. The colony is on the verge of atmospheric collapse. I'm the technology director and I must prevent a catastrophe." Furthermore, she needed to rescue Cody from the Matchmaker's men.

"I know who you used to be, Shim Neesa." Mr. Praetorius did not alter his course. "Now answer my questions. What caused the wreck?"

Lisa's body responded to more of her commands. She adjusted her position along his side to make a little space between them. She'd recently learned that someone had been interpreting her family's private conversations for the government her whole life.

"Do you speak Korean?" She withheld all traces of accusation from her tone out of caution.

"Yes, I do." He spoke in Korean. "Now tell me how my master died."

Curiously, the language shift altered the meaning of the word from husband to master. "Were you enslaved?" She found the concept chilling because the Matchmaker had only moments ago stripped her elite status and declared her a slave in the breeding program.

"Answer my question." Mr. Praetorius' body tensed, straining the seams of his suit.

"I can't." The neural implant behind her ear would transmit every word, prompting swift retaliation. "They'll know."

"You're chipped?" He growled as he flipped off the comm switch.

Accelerating the craft, he adjusted course. Instead of heading north, he piloted the rover north westward. Since he'd cut off communication, she didn't ask any more stupid questions.

Chapter Four

Space Division Agent Cody Greene awoke to the rasp of a zipper and a sense of lingering betrayal. The bitter smell of a sanitizing solution hung in the air. His mother had confessed that she could no longer protect him from her father's breeding program right before she'd jabbed him with a sedative.

He preferred death to exploitation and vowed to bring the Matchmaker to justice. Fully conscious, he forced open his heavy eyelids, shifted on the narrow gurney, and winced at a shooting pain in his backside. Had he injured his tailbone when he'd passed out?

Within the windowless medical bay of a large transport vehicle, a dark-haired woman in a red Health Division uniform stood beside the bed opposite of him rapidly taping the screen of a hand held datapad.

Even facing away, she looked familiar. Why was his brain so sluggish? His eidetic memory should have identified her immediately.

She slapped the device on the gurney in front of her, bracing both hands on the edge of the bed with her head down. Cold and wearing nothing but a hospital gown, Cody swung his legs over the side and sat upright, taking care not to expose his body. Hidden cameras often recorded spaces like this.

The woman faced him, causing the curls of her high ponytail to bounce. "Forgive me, Mr. Greene." She clutched her arms to her chest.

"Where are we headed, Director Tran?" He found the defensive reaction odd coming from a superior.

"We're bound for TEN." Andrea Tran tucked her uniform top into the waistband of her slacks.

"Where's Lisa?" Cody raised his eyebrows, searching his memory for an explanation.

"Ask Counselor Albright." Andrea clenched her jaw.

"What does my mother have to do with my wife?" Cody's course of thought faltered.

"I'm not at liberty to say." Andrea stubbornly avoided his gaze.

"What's wrong with me?" He swayed under the lingering effects of the injection.

"I'm sorry, Cody." Andrea took a half-step backward and bumped into the gurney behind her. "I can't refuse orders and expect to live. I provided her with a sedative in a syringe, and she dosed you. It's affecting your memory."

"You helped her betray me?" Cody's anger swelled within his chest.

Andrea's posture slumped as lines of grief pinched around her eyes. She gathered underclothes and a red uniform from a duffel bag next to the datapad. Her hands trembled as she laid them beside him.

"I'll leave you to dress." She strode toward the forward-facing hatch.

The transport halted abruptly, sending Cody and Andrea crashing against the bulkhead leading to the passenger compartment. They collided, ending up in a pile of loose objects. Fortunately, the gurneys had stayed clamped to the deck plating.

"Did we hit something?" Andrea brusquely shoved him off her.

"No." Buffeted but otherwise uninjured, Cody dressed quickly.

A stop like that meant danger. He glanced at the readings on the door controls. Atmospheric pressure filled the other side of the bulkhead. A good sign.

Andrea stood and keyed in the door code to enter the passenger cabin. Cody zipped his slacks and buttoned his top as he followed her. His actions caught his mother's attention in the cabin's second row of chairs.

"You'd better strap into the pilot's seat." Addison Albright looked away from her son to face forward with a tense expression barely visible in the dim lighting. "Ours is dead."

Cody and Andrea strode along the aisle between passenger seats to the man slumped in a five-point harness. Black marks seared the sides of his head. Cody's stomach lurched.

Andrea placed two fingertips at his neck. "No pulse."

Cody searched for a cause. The window panels on either side of the pilot's seat had holes sealed with gel, preventing the atmosphere from escaping. He'd never seen anything like it.

The dark of night surrounded them with an enemy lurking within it. "You should both suit up." Cody hefted the dead man from the seat and took his place, accelerating the transport along the Glass Highway.

"The revolution won't last long." Addison didn't make a move to put on an environmental suit. "The outlaws don't have enough resources."

"Why would outlaws take a shot at a medical transport?" Cody couldn't see anything beyond the headlights' range.

"We encroached on their territory five years ago." Addison sighed. "They said it was an act of war, and have mounted an active resistance ever since."

"Why did we—" A brilliant flash of light ahead seized Cody's attention.

Chaotic laser fire illuminated the rocky, Martian landscape. On the northern side of the highway, Space Division assault vehicles raced toward outlaw personnel in environmental suits. Bursts of explosive energy burned the oxygen inside a craft or a suit until snuffed out by the near vacuum of the planet's less than one percent atmospheric pressure.

"We need to assist the wounded." Cody's emergency medical training kicked in.

"No, don't stop for any reason." Addison's face creased with worry lines.

"We can save stranded people from exposure to the cold." Andrea Tran stripped her clothes and worked her way into an environmental suit.

"No." Addison met Cody's gaze in the rear-view mirror. "Keep driving, Son. There should be plenty of support vehicles reserved for the battle's aftermath."

Cody ground his teeth as he piloted the transport past the conflict. "Why aren't we dead?" He glanced at the corpse beside him on the deck. "This transport should be venting atmosphere." The punctured side windows turned from clear to opaque.

"We're perfectly safe." Addison waved her hand as if to dismiss his concern. "Your wife is an ingenious engineer, and this is her latest prototype."

"It's true." Andrea sealed her suit's gauntlets. "Lisa started working on self-sealing panels after your rover wreck last month, Mr. Greene." Andrea grabbed her helmet. "However, each panel only seals one breach. If we're hit again in the same panel, then we'll explosively decompress. I suggest you follow my lead, Counselor Albright."

An enormous blast of laser fire vaporized holes through a row of outlaws cresting a hilltop on the horizon. The figures erupted in flames. Past trauma caused bile to rise in Cody's throat.

"There's no longer a need for concern." Addison clenched her jaw.

"How can you be certain?" Andrea clutched a helmet to her chest.

"That blast came from Laser Outpost Juliet." Cody's mother's head bowed. "If we're within line of sight, then the Space Division will fire on all resistance craft and personnel."

"Where's Lisa?" Cody interjected with the only question that mattered.

"I'm sorry, Son." Addison met his gaze in the rear-view mirror with a tortured look in her eyes. "I've been informed that it's too late for her."

Cody clutched the controls, swerving to avoid a burned-out rover on the highway. The transport launched onto the desert floor, and he did his best to keep it from colliding with a boulder. Pumping the brakes, he ground the craft to a halt.

"What do you mean?" His heart pounded in his chest. "Where is she?"

"A radio call came in soon after our departure." Addison's lips turned downward at the corners. "Mr. Praetorius took Lisa half an hour ago."

"She can't be gone." Cody's mind stalled, unwilling to accept the possibility of losing her.

"Praetorius executed her bodyguards and tortured the Matchmaker." Addison grasped her seat's armrests. "Only one set of tracks left the ocean habitat's airlock. Since we can't find Lisa or her environmental suit, it looks like he hauled her away. Given the attack we're under, there isn't anyone available to pursue them."

"I'll go after her." Cody accelerated the transport across the open desert in a northwesterly direction. "I can intercept the assassin before he enters the Northern Territories."

"He took her, Cody." Addison met his gaze wide eyed in the low light. "There's no saving either of them now."

"Took her how?" Cody stared into the rear-view mirror at his mother, but she avoided his gaze, so he turned to Andrea. "Tell me."

"It doesn't look good." Andrea broke her attention away from Addison to meet his gaze. "The investigators retrieved a sample of seminal fluid from the catwalk in the ocean habitat. They also reported finding a lot of blood."

"Whose blood?" Cody focused on the terrain.

"That's unclear." Andrea's voice held a great deal of tension. "NINE is in crisis. Lisa initiated emergency protocols and warned the other colonies of an impending collapse. My staff has sealed the sub-level two hospital as an emergency shelter. They had time thanks to Lisa's quick actions."

"And you're here." Cody growled. "Why is that, Director Tran? Why aren't you helping the colonists?"

Andrea cringed. His mother avoided his gaze altogether. This couldn't be happening.

"I'm under orders." Andrea's shoulders curled inward. "I didn't have a choice."

"Sure." Cody scoffed. "So much for loyalty."

"Lisa is my best friend." Andrea's gaze snapped to meet his. "I'll do whatever it takes to help her. Councilor Albright granted me access to resources I need to find a cure for Rotcargathogen. It's Lisa's only hope."

"What?" Cody stared at the director. "Lisa has the Rot?"

"Maybe." Andrea squared her shoulders. "All we've learned for sure is that the executioner is infected."

"But–" Cody's chest seized with anguish. "There's no cure for the Rot."

"I will find one." Andrea stood, holding the headrest of the seat in front of her for balance in the jostling craft. "You have my word."

"You'd better keep it, but first we're going to rescue her." Cody ignored his mother's quiet sobs.

Chapter Five

The megalithic landscape of Mars at night towered above the stealth rover as Royce piloted it north. He and Lisa shivered uncontrollably in each others arms, seeking survival despite their former enmity. Life support at minimal, the environmental suits they wore offered little protection as the temperature outside the unsealed and poorly shielded craft dropped by the hour.

"Take me back, Mr. Praetorius." The vibrations of her voice transferred from her helmet to his.

"My name is Royce Nedge." A primal urge not to lose her sprang up within him. "And I'll never give you back to that monster."

The last of the power drained from the low to the ground rover's batteries. In the starlight, the solar panels didn't help much, and the ripple tracks crawled to a halt. At the same time, the navigation screen blinked out.

Royce slammed the console as Lisa pushed open the wrap around solar panels. Gravity finished the process, forcing the panels to lay flat on the sand beside the craft. He unplugged their suits from the useless oxygen recycling system and nonfunctional heater.

Standing, he pulled her up in front of him to touch helmets. "We have three minutes of air, but we can make it before we freeze if we run."

"Lead the way." Though in shadow, she held his gaze.

He nodded and jumped over the solar panels, running fast toward a beacon on the nearest bluff despite the pain in his groin. She trailed behind him crossing the sand into a split in the butte. Her white environmental suit disappeared from his view when he rounded a curve.

Panting for air, he redoubled his efforts. His suit had no power for lights. Regardless, he hastened forward with his shoulders scraping against the red sandstone until he found the hatch.

Freezing to death, he wrestled with the wheel to unseal the emergency shelter. Lisa's helmet bumped into his elbow. She immediately slid behind him and wrapped her arms around his middle.

Her warmth and the intimacy of her touch encouraged him to struggle hard enough to break the wheel loose. It turned. Swinging the hatch open, he dragged Lisa inside and resealed it.

Holding her against his shivering body for warmth, he hit the red button glowing in the dark. Pressurized air filled the equalizing chamber. He stepped away from her as a rinse of warm, sanitizing solution decontaminated the exteriors of their suits, draining into the grating at their feet.

Dim lighting switched on in the small airlock. He unsealed his helmet and gauntlets, placing them on the deck as he ran a hand through the short-cropped hair on his head. Lisa glanced at the controls that vacuumed air from the chamber.

"Go ahead if that's what you plan to do." He knew she could hear the vibrations of his voice through the air despite the helmet she wore.

"I'm not a killer." She pried open the seals on her helmet and retrieved her glasses from where they'd slid below her chin.

"But I am, so you think I deserve to die." He swept her long, black hair behind her right ear, tracing the fresh scar he found there. "They're listening to everything you say." He shook his head. "I shouldn't be surprised. Anyway, the rock shields the signal. You can speak freely about what happened to Alik and the others."

"I wanted to tell you before, but it wasn't safe." She let out a heavy sigh. "I should have said, I'm sorry for your loss, though."

"I don't need your condolences." He adjusted his stance to a more relaxed pose. "I need answers."

"And I need to return to NINE so I can save the colonists." She lifted her chin to meet his gaze.

"The colonists are fine for a while." He leaned his back against the wall, avoiding her supple, feminine curves and the way his pulse rate responded to them. "The Matchmaker can't leave NINE until he's sufficiently recovered. He's probably still in emergency surgery."

Lisa met his gaze. "Why didn't you kill him?"

"I was about to, but he escaped." Royce clenched his jaw. "Now, tell me what I want to know."

"If he can't be moved, then NINE is safe." She closed her eyes, catching her breath. "All right, the wreck last month left our rover upside down. With Cody unconscious and the driver mortally wounded, I dropped from my harness and tried to seal the cracked observation bubble. Unfortunately, I couldn't do much until I righted the vehicle. So, I rocked it over onto its wheels." Her voice quavered. "I didn't realize it then, but it crushed a blonde woman outside. I found her dead when the Space Division soldiers rescued us. She must have been approaching on foot."

"And what of my husband?" Royce had mourned over Shade's tragically crushed body along with the others brought back when what was left of the scrapyard crew had returned with the wreckage.

"The rescuers destroyed a small craft with laser fire as they came in." Lisa glanced at him. "And there was a man lying on the side of the road amidst a scattering of rock fragments. His environmental suit had torn on impact with the rover." A tremor shook her body. "I think he caused the crash by pushing a large stone into our path. Why would he do that?"

"Improvisation." Royce had heard this much from Addison. "Shade broke the electromagnetic pulse weapon."

"I saw no evidence of a helicopter drone." Lisa frowned.

"It's not a drone." He eyed her severely. "It's a roadside device triggered by motion sensors to disable a passing vehicle."

"The rover still had power." She adjusted her glasses on her nose. "I checked on the outlaw to see if I could help him, but he'd died instantly. Then I inspected the Glass Highway for damage. I probably would have noticed a device capable of knocking out a rover. Well, possibly. It was dark, and I was in a state of mild shock. I could have missed it."

"Shade screwed everything up." Royce had always pitied her nervousness. "She tinkered with equipment, trying to improve it, but she ended up breaking it instead." He grieved just thinking about her. "It's exactly like Alik to come up with a work around after the plan failed."

"The rock was effective." Lisa rubbed her temples. "Though an electromagnetic pulse would have been gentler."

"That's an understatement." Royce noticed her tight expression. "Does the chip give you headaches?" He resisted the urge to massage her neck, knowing that every time he touched her his ability to distance himself from her eroded.

"It's a neural-mesh implant." She grimaced. "If they overload it, then I'll die."

"And you don't want that to happen." He gently grasped her head and inspected the scar more closely. "I've never heard of a neural implant. How can it be removed if it has meshed with your brain?"

"It can't." She shied away from his touch. "I was a fool to invent it."

"As usual." He scoffed, letting his hands fall to his sides. "You know what this means, right?"

"Yes." Tears burst from her eyes followed by sobs that shook her narrow shoulders. "I can never go home."

"This isn't about you anymore." He attempted to pace in the tight space without success.

"Unless–" She removed her gauntlets and wiped the moisture from her cheeks. "Unless the signal is blocked." An intensely thoughtful expression overwhelmed her facial features. "Or jammed." She met his gaze. "I can invent a way around this problem."

"Right." He tapped the side of her head. "But, you're not the only one they're going to put this thing in. How are you going to save the whole planet from their domination?"

She stared up at him, chest heaving for breath as her jaw hung slightly ajar. Then she shook her head and started hyperventilating. Covering her mouth with a hand, she slid down the wall to sit on the deck grating.

"It was only meant to be a communications device." She panted. "They're the ones who added a tracker. Now the power drain makes it dangerous."

"I'm guessing." He squatted beside her and lifted her chin. "That you never imagined they would abuse your invention in this way."

"I did it to help people, not to hurt them." A tormented look creased the delicate skin around her eyes.

"It's sad." His heart ached for the sorrow he'd seen inflicted on countless victims by the things she'd invented to help people. "You don't even know what you've done."

"What?" She paled.

"They've twisted every idea you've ever had." He knew what they were hiding inside the Incursion Zone, at least, he thought he did. "Your visionary mind is the reason the colonists lives are at risk. But now I have you and they don't. So, maybe something good will come of you yet."

A wounded look overcame her confused expression. He sat opposite of her, legs touching because there wasn't enough space. She'd lost everyone she loved, her freedom, and her elite status to the Matchmaker all in one day. Royce almost sympathized enough to offer physical comfort.

Chapter Six

Lisa awoke propped in the corner with Royce's head on her lap. Sometime in the early morning, he must have plugged the refresh hose into her suit because the completion chime had awakened her when the cycle concluded. A pouch of water had partially filled inside the unit.

That was her recycled liquid. Pressing her lips together in distaste, she detached the pouch and drank it without disturbing the sleeping man scrunched on the cramped deck grating. If the empty pouch on the floor was any indication, then he'd already drank his water.

Perhaps, she'd earned his trust. She would need his cooperation to fulfill her plan to save Cody from the Matchmaker and ensure the safety of the colonists from the Gold Council. She stared at the face of the man who held so many lives in his hands.

Asleep, he looked like a high school aged version of Cody. The observation disturbed her deeply. Rubbing her sore neck, she tried not to think of how Royce Nedge had strangled her three weeks ago and left her in a coma.

Assassins did that kind of thing. Fortunately for her, he'd changed his mind and rescued her from enslavement. Assassins didn't usually do that sort of thing, did they?

"No, no, please..." Royce tensed in his sleep. "Don't..."

Without thinking, she stroked the hair from his forehead with her fingertips. "You're all right." She pulled her hand away in shock, not having meant to touch the man.

He relaxed and continued sleeping. Her seven, younger siblings often had nightmares, and this is what she'd done to soothe them. It was second nature, but she'd never imagined she'd be assuaging a killer's guilty conscience with the technique.

She glanced at the chronometer on the simple control panel. Six fifty-three, the stealth rover would have power soon. Her stomach growled uncomfortably.

The last time she'd eaten had been at the awards brunch yesterday in NINE. It was her final meal with Cody. At least she'd used her concluding hours of freedom with him to count for something amazing.

"You sigh a lot." Royce stirred and looked up at her. "You even do it in your sleep." He sat up, rubbing his beardless face.

"How old are you?" She hadn't realized she'd started grieving for Cody, but she had.

"I'm thirty-two months shy of your age." He grabbed his helmet and gauntlets from the deck.

"You look younger." Lisa had finished high school a long time ago. "Do you have family in the colonies?"

"I had Alik, Shade, and my friends." He sealed his suit.

"I'm sorry." She mourned with him. "Thank you for saving me from the Matchmaker."

Royce nodded, detached the refresh hose from her suit, and stowed it while she sealed her gauntlets and helmet. He hit the button to vacuum the air, and the two of them stepped out into the crevasse. The rock was a gorgeous color of dark red sandstone.

It reminded her of Cody's choice of hand massage stone back when they'd just moved to NINE and were sitting through endless meetings with her staff. She would endure a thousand days as tedious as that one for a chance to be in the same room with him again. Royce resealed the hatch and headed through the crevasse toward the stealth rover.

She followed him until he stopped near the opening. With apparent caution, he surveyed the wide area beyond. Nothing stood out as dangerous in her estimation.

She might have asked him any number of questions if he hadn't removed the communications modules from the suits back in NINE. She knew why he'd done it. They contained tracking devices, and he hadn't wanted to be followed.

Unfortunately, he hadn't realized that she was a tracking device. Anyway, her questions could wait until they were in the rover. Once they were attached to life support, they'd be able to communicate again.

He raised a hand to stop her. Glancing once more at the lay of the land, he started running. She stayed hidden in the crevasse.

Slogging through the sand didn't seem to slow him down. Once at the rover, he activated the controls, raised the camouflaging solar panels, and piloted the craft toward her. She hurried to climb inside as soon as he opened up to let her in.

The craft concealed their stark white suits from view. Royce piloted the ripple tracks of the rover over the footprints they'd left behind. The craft left no trace that either it or they had traveled this way.

"It's a remarkable vehicle." Lisa spoke as soon as they were both plugged into the life support system. "I was invited to be a part of the design team, but I declined."

"It has a singular military purpose." He accelerated across a stretch of flat ground.

"Exactly." She adjusted her body to put a little space between the two of them in the tight seat. "What need does anyone have for stealth except for one colony to spy on another, and I couldn't condone that. Of course, I hadn't realized there were outlaws back then. Nor had I suspected that the government was completely corrupt."

"The innocent never suspect the wicked until it's too late." His voice took on a note of sorrow. "Now, you're depending on an outlaw and a stealth rover for survival."

"I was such a fool." Her recrimination came as guilt landed squarely on her shoulders. "Cody was wiser. But then, he was an undercover agent and knew better. I was an engineer, and my life was simpler."

"Cody was a spy?" Royce glanced at her. "I should have guessed. Everything makes more sense now. But, your life isn't over. You're still an engineer. That's not a simple thing. Your inventions are extremely complex."

"Maybe." She shook her head. "But with machines the components function predictably to create the whole. Unfortunately, I don't understand people nearly as well."

"You're pragmatic." Royce gazed at the stark landscape ahead. "Most people aren't like that. Regardless, your compliance didn't save you from the Matchmaker any more than mine saved me."

Stricken, she considered his words. "Maybe so, but Cody's scepticism didn't prevent his exploitation either." She grieved for what the modest man she loved must be going through.

"We've all been manipulated." Royce's gauntlet curled into a fist. "I should have snapped the Matchmaker's neck when I had the chance."

She had a hard time disagreeing.

Chapter Seven

Cody blamed his mother for everything. It was a bad habit left over from his childhood. But she had surprised him by not arguing about endangering her life going after Lisa.

Instead, she had helped Andrea drag the dead pilot to the medical bay in a body bag. Afterward, she'd settled in a passenger seat and fallen asleep. Not once had she played the pampered politician or demanded that he return to a colony.

Cody drove the medical rover throughout the night. When they reached a good vantage point on a bluff, he deployed a camouflaging blind. Watching the vista below, he used the craft's thermal imaging sensors to detect approaching vehicles.

Long-range cameras showed no fresh tracks of any kind other than on the border patrol road. This remote stretch of desert was the safest place for a fugitive to cross into the Northern Territories. Why hadn't Praetorius come?

"The sun's up." Andrea Tran unbuckled and strode forward to peer out the front window. "Any sign of Lisa?"

"No, not yet, and they should be here by now." A shiver traversed Cody's spine. "Do you think they froze to death?"

Andrea shook her head. "The assassin must have had a plan. Otherwise, he wouldn't have gone outside the bio-dome at night."

"He's smart." Cody considered the problem. "He might have gone back into the colony through another airlock. But they were looking for him, and he knew about the air and water loss. No, he wouldn't go inside. If he called for help, then someone may have picked him and Lisa up. Was there a report of any unauthorized radio chatter?"

Andrea frowned as she sat in a front row passenger seat. "The colony police didn't say."

"Then, he must have had a vehicle hidden within walking distance because he had to hike in somehow and would have needed a way to escape." Cody rubbed the stubble on his jaw. "But where could they have gone?"

"Do you think he joined the battle?" Andrea leaned forward.

"Lisa would do her duty." On impulse, Cody pressed a button to retract the blind in preparation to set the medical rover in motion. "NINE was her responsibility. She must have struck a bargain with her captor to stop the flow of resources out of the colonies. She'll go to an access hatch and shut the valves."

"Wait." Andrea stood. "I don't think Lisa is in a position to negotiate. If you're sure this is the most likely place, then we can't leave until we've verified that they aren't coming."

"I hope you're wrong." Cody hated the logic of her words, it meant that Lisa was powerless, and that wasn't something he was accustomed to.

He monitored the scanners in the transport. The sun rose higher in the yellow hued sky. His mother awakened, but didn't interfere in his search.

"What's that?" Andrea pointed out the front window at a distant dust trail swirling on the desert floor.

"It could be a dirt devil." He zoomed in on it with the cameras.

"It's camouflaged and moving north." Andrea clapped him on the shoulder. "But its dust is blowing east."

"Looks like a stealth rover." He started the medical rover on an intercept course.

Worrying that they were farther ahead of him than he'd expected, he put the medical rover in all-terrain mode and barreled the bulky craft along the patrol road. Despite his consummate skill, the transport struggled to catch up with the ripple-track rover. He needed to cut the assassin off, and that would take a level of daring that only his love for Lisa could muster.

"What are you doing?" Addison slammed against the five-point harness that kept her head from splattering on the deck plating like a cracked egg.

"Sorry, Mother, but there's no help for it." Cody accelerated, launching the craft across a chasm to land on a lower tier of the terrace of red rock along the canyon wall.

"We haven't crossed the border yet, have we?" Andrea cinched her restraints tighter and held onto the armrests white-knuckled.

"No." He shook his head. "That ridge is the geographic marker. The assassin is heading for a cleft in the rocks. I'm going to block the gap before he can escape."

"Are you going to stop if they make it first?" Andrea paled despite her Asian complexion.

"No." His mother answered the question. "He won't, and I can't blame him. It's not in his nature to give up on family."

Her firm tone held surety with a hint of something else, maybe pride. He wondered if she were secretly pleased with him, and hoped she was. Regardless, neither she nor anyone else had the power to stop him, not here in the wilds where he'd always been free.

The ripple-track rover's pilot shifted out of stealth mode and raced toward the gap in the ridge. Its occupants must have spotted the medical rover. Lisa's life depended on Cody reaching the divide in the rocks first.

Against his better judgment, he engaged the emergency power source and plowed through the sandy terrain. Small rocks bounced from the nose of the craft. The front window cracked at the far-right corner, but the sealing gel prevented a total failure. It congealed, spreading through the bent and separating transparent aluminum. Lisa's innovation had saved their lives for a second time.

"Slow down." Andrea's wide eyes stared at a boulder in their path.

"We only have one chance." He avoided it, smashing into a dune that sprayed the vehicle with splotches of red sand.

The console speaker crackled to life. "Medical Rover Prototype Eleven, we see you and are on an intercept course."

In the far distance, an assault vehicle kicked up dust on the desert floor, rapidly closing in on the gap in the ridge. Cody didn't ease up, not even when they launched a drone. He couldn't afford to lose the love of his life just when he'd finally given her his heart.

The camouflaged solar panels concealed the occupants of the stealth rover, but the helmet of a passenger emerged from between them. Lisa captured Cody's gaze from a distance as her lips moved with speech he couldn't hear. He memorized their every movement, groaning because he'd missed the opportunity to cut off the rover.

"Follow your brother through." Addison leaned forward in her seat.

Cody swung in behind Lisa and the assassin as they shot through the gap. Just then, a helicopter drone descended right in front of the ripple-track rover, surged over it, and emitted an electromagnetic pulse, knocking out the electronics of the medical rover. It rolled to a pathetic stop, and Cody slammed the dead instruments with his palms.

Praetorius and Lisa sped ahead in a cloud of dust. The assault vehicles had taken the medical rover out instead of the ripple-track. He'd been betrayed again.

"You did this." Cody popped the harness and stood to face his mother in anger, furious at the mention of a brother that couldn't exist.

She sat lifeless in her seat. Andrea followed his line of sight. The two of them reacted simultaneously to render aid.

"Her heart's stopped beating." Andrea had two fingers at Addison's neck.

Cody unbuckled his mother and laid her in the aisle of the rover, beginning chest compressions. Andrea removed his mother's wedding band and stroked it upward behind Addison's right ear, tracing a fresh incision. Then, she administered mouth to mouth resuscitation.

"Why isn't it working?" Andrea sprang to her feet and manually cranked the door open, running for a kit from the medical bay. "This might help." She returned to inject a syringe of adrenaline into Addison's heart.

Nothing happened. Cody continued chest compressions. A thump on the front window of the rover drew his attention for a split second.

Praetorius in a white environmental suit stood pounding on the window with the heel of a fist. Cody ignored the threat of the stun rifle in his brother's other hand and focused on reviving his mother. Praetorius watched everything with a look of intense distress.

Suddenly, the medical rover shifted, jostled by the impact of a craft docking with it. Cody's hopes of escape died, but he kept working on his mother. Andrea had nothing in her medical kit to help since the defibrillator wouldn't work after the electromagnetic pulse knocked it out along with everything else.

The rear hatch swung open and armed soldiers stormed into the medical bay. Praetorius stared at the men. Lisa joined him to look into the rover.

Her gauntlet splayed on the window. She made eye contact with Cody for the split second he could spare from trying to save his mother's life. Glancing her way again, Cody saw her grab Praetorius and touch her helmet to his for direct voice communication.

"You can't save the councilor." A soldier leveled his laser rifle on Praetorius outside the front window. "The electromagnetic pulse triggered her kill switch. Now, move into the assault vehicle so I can shoot that outlaw."

Cody swept his mother's blonde hair away from her right ear to inspect the small wound behind it. Furious, he kept up chest compressions. Lisa's neural-mesh implant had killed her.

A second soldier pointed a stun pistol at his head. Andrea dove for her helmet, but Cody couldn't give up on his mother. The pulse dropped him like a stone.

Chapter Eight

Royce and Lisa watched two Space Division soldiers haul Cody's unconscious body to the docked assault vehicle. Andrea Tran swept the hair away from behind Addison's right ear, and ran the metal circle up the small pink scar. She continued with chest compressions until the soldiers dragged her into the assault craft.

Royce pulled Lisa down before the soldiers returned. After a few minutes, the men departed in their assault vehicle. The drone lay drained of power on the sand.

Royce picked it up and smashed it against the front of the medical rover. Stepping up on the bumper, he stared into the vehicle. Addison's lifeless body lay in the aisle.

Lisa stepped up beside him, grabbed him by the shoulder, and pressed her helmet to his. Her words didn't register in his mind, but the tone of condolence made his mother's death real. Even so, he watched his mother's body for any sign of life.

"I won't let them have her." He ran to the ripple-track.

Reversing it, he attached a cable to the medical rover and pulled the large craft into the Northern Territories. Lisa followed on foot as he towed the medical rover behind a boulder. Still visible from the gap, he climbed up and deployed the craft's camouflaging blind.

Had the electromagnetic pulse taken Addison's life via an implant? If so, then the Matchmaker had ordered the assassination and used Lisa's invention to murder his own daughter. Addison had known she would die and she hadn't cared as long as her sons were freed.

Unfortunately, she'd failed. Cody wasn't free, and there was nothing Royce could do to save his brother now. He met Lisa's gaze, and the two of them boarded the ripple-track, covering any trace of the medical rover before setting off for safety.

He sent out a coded message to the scrapyard crew for a recovery mission, siting the location and the value of the craft. With his last abilities, he piloted them away from the tragedy. His mother had died for him, yet he'd never had a chance to know her well.

Lisa plugged in the life support lines, reaching over to flip on the communications. Royce listened to her soft breaths. Somehow, saying nothing, melted through his defenses faster than anything she could have said.

He broke down into raucous sobs. Lisa took his gauntleted free hand in hers as a line of confusion creased her delicate brow. He surrendered to his grief all the more for seeing it.

"That woman was my mother." Royce didn't know how to explain the flood of emotions that were nearly crippling him right now.

"I'm so sorry to hear that." Lisa hugged him around the shoulders, resting her helmet against his neck. "I had no idea you were Addison Albright's son?"

"What do you know about her?" He had so many questions.

"She's a member of the Gold Council and the head administrator for NINE." Lisa took a deep breath and let it out slowly. "I've never met her, but she gives political speeches often enough that everyone knows of her."

Royce hated being lied to. "You must know her better than that." Fury raised in his chest.

"No." Lisa stiffened. "She appointed me tech director, but that's the only connection I have. It was done without discussion. I was compelled to agree or my sister would never return from an assignment in TEN. I haven't sought the councilor's favor."

"Cody never spoke of her?" Royce clenched his fist.

"Never." Lisa shook her head. "I don't think he knows her. Though, he and Andrea were doing their best to revive her."

"Why do you think he was with her?" Royce had seen how much Cody loved their mother. "She must be someone close to him." Why wouldn't Lisa admit the connection?

"I can't explain it." Lisa's expression saddened. "Cody wasn't allowed to tell me the truth about many things."

"Why?" Royce clenched his jaw.

"Undercover agents are obliged to keep secrets." She shook her head. "I had hoped that was all over with when he timed out, but they were still constraining him."

The pieces clicked together in Royce's mind. "Addison manipulated you into redeeming Cody from a death sentence by threatening your sister, right?"

"Yes, it looks that way." Lisa sighed. "Cody was commissioned to investigate me for resource theft, but I didn't do it." A brief smile softened her grief stricken features. "Despite all of his lies and the government's manipulations, we fell in love."

"You love Cody Greene?" Royce ground his teeth in torment. "Even after he raped you?"

"He did no such thing." She stared at him wide eyed. "Why would you think so?"

"Because of the damage." Royce pointed between her legs. "Tearing like that doesn't happen during a loving encounter."

Lisa cringed. "He didn't mean to hurt me, but he's large."

"And you're not." Royce remembered the communications technicians and their heat sensor video.

"It was our first time." Lisa turned away. "You can't blame my husband for not knowing what to do."

"Husband?" Royce's heartbeat faltered for an instant. "You talk as if the Matchmaker didn't dissolve your legal status, including your marriage, the instant he brought you two into the breeding program."

Lisa gasped. "My marriage has been dissolved?"

"Yes." Royce stared straight ahead at the undulating terrain. "And I have salvage rights over you." The second part was a lie, but since no one knew he was a clone, he could still claim to be human.

"What does that mean?" Lisa's voice held a deeply disapproving tone.

"The instant we crossed the border, you became part of my holdings." His hoarse voice grated like gravel inside his helmet. "The law requires you to obey me or die. They call it husbandry because I feed and shelter you."

"I call it slavery." Her breathing rate increased to the point of hyperventilation. "You will never be my husband."

"I am your master." He spoke Korean as he wrapped an arm around her and dragged her against his side.

"God is my master." She stiffened but didn't fight him.

"Will you serve me?" He agreed with her, but the law required her compliance.

"I will help you do anything that is good." She steadied her breathing.

"Then, that's what I will ask of you." He eased his hold on her, soothed by the softness of her reply. "Now, tell me everything you know of Addison Albright." His heart ached for the loss of the mother he'd loved his whole life, yet never spent more than a few minutes with.

Chapter Nine

Cody languished in an outpost prison cell. His mother had died, and his last words to her had been spoken in anger. Everything about the way she'd acted and the things she'd said indicated that she knew the Matchmaker would kill her for going after Lisa and Praetorius.

Yet, she'd gone without complaint, perhaps because the assassin was her son. Sitting on the edge of a cot, Cody held his head in his hands in agony. At least, this time there was no leaky faucet to torment him.

He scoffed at the despicable pettiness of the thought, stood, and weakly paced the cell that for some reason felt tippy turvy beneath his bare feet. He'd been stunned, but that should have worn off quickly. No, there was more to his present state of unwell than a stun-gun blast.

He'd been drugged. The pain in his backside had spread to his groin, twinging with every step. Furthermore, his thoughts wandered, lacking focus.

The dark suspicion that these symptoms were somehow connected oppressed him. What did it mean to be in the breeding program without his wife? The Matchmaker could have killed Lisa as easily as he had murdered Addison, but instead he had allowed Praetorius to escape with the woman Cody loved.

He stumbled to the cot and lay on his side. Unlike two months ago, this time he hadn't been given any clothing. A glint of paranoia surfaced, and he looked over the cell for anywhere a camera might be concealed.

It wasn't hidden. There in the upper corner, mounted directly facing him was a high quality video camera. He rolled over to face the wall, wishing he had a blanket.

The key turned in the cell door. Cody ducked onto his stomach to conceal as much of his body as possible. In walked Andrea Tran in her red Health Division uniform and Holden Martin in his silver-gray Space Division jumpsuit.

Embarrassment overwhelmed Cody as his jumbled emotions flushed his skin. Andrea was a doctor and the sight of his naked backside didn't seem to distract her. However, Holden's gaze fixated in an openly interested manner that showed unabashed approval. It was just like when they were roommates at the Space Academy, and Cody hated it.

"Are you feeling any better?" Andrea met his gaze.

"Would you like to?" Holden leered openly.

"I'd like a uniform." Cody ignored Holden's tone.

"You need a blood draw and a physical first." Andrea reached into the hallway for a medical cart.

"Please, ask him to leave." Cody's anger at the indignity surged.

"He's my husband and serving as your guard." She put on a pair of latex gloves.

"But he's not interested in women." Cody used the pillow as a shield to cover his groin and sat on the edge of the cot.

"And I'm not usually interested in men, but the match was made." Andrea sterilized the crook of Cody's arm and felt for his vein. "You'll feel a small pinch." She stuck his vein with a needle and filled five vials with blood before removing it and taping a cotton swab to the wound.

"Are you part of a foursome?" Cody frowned in concentration, trying to understand how the Marriage Mandate and four child requirements under colonial law could be fulfilled with a couple who weren't inclined toward one another unless this rare exception had been made on their behalf.

"Yes." Holden stepped forward, but Andrea held him back.

"That remains to be seen." She met Holden's gaze. "We're waiting for a legal resolution. There has been a complication."

"Oh." Cody pitied their situation. "Lisa said you married five months ago, but she never said anything about your preferences." Lisa and Andrea had been best friends since junior high school.

"We're compliant." Holden scowled. "Don't trouble yourself over me."

"Oh." Cody glanced at Andrea's flat stomach, but looked away when color flushed her cheeks.

"Despite our compliance, pregnancy has proved a challenge." Andrea frowned. "Please, remove the pillow so I can examine you."

"Have him turn away." Cody stood with his back to the camera, but kept the pillow in place.

"Fine." Holden sullenly complied.

"Thank you." Andrea fetched a short, round stool on wheels from the hallway and used it to examine his most intimate places. "Everything seems in order, but that doesn't explain the problem." She reached for the medical cart again, retrieving a cup and a small remote control. "Please, provide a sample for analysis."

"Urine?" Cody had endured more humiliation in the last five minutes than in his entire life.

"Semen." Andrea proffered him the cup, holding the small remote in her other hand.

"No." Cody reached for the pillow, covering his private area. "It's against my religion to relinquish control of my reproductive material."

"They know that." Holden adjusted his stance but didn't look in Cody's direction. "Comply or die. That's how it is." He almost sounded sorry.

"I choose death, then." Cody battled the upset building in his chest and the inability to catch his breath in this weakened condition.

"No one wants that, Cody." Andrea guided him to sit on the edge of the cot. "We're only confirming a suspicion anyway."

"What?" His pulse pounded in his temples.

"It looks like you're sterile." Andrea touched his shoulder, meeting his gaze. "Lisa's compliance exam indicated the probability, but with all of the confusion in NINE, we just received the results."

"I can't have children?" Cody hunched over the pillow, hugging it in distress.

"I'm sterile too." Holden came to sit beside him on the cot with a heavy sigh. "It isn't as bad as you think, though it complicates marriage relationships."

"Yes, it does, but Cody's situation isn't certain yet." Andrea wheeled her chair directly in front of him, holding the cup and the remote in her hands. "Please, let me see if there's anything that can be done to help you."

Cody glanced at Holden. He nodded and went to stand outside the cell, closing the door almost completely. Cody trembled in dread at the thought of compelling his body to give this type of sample.

"I've never done this before." His hands turned cold. "My religion prohibits self-stimulation."

"Take a deep breath, this will hurt a little." She set the remote control on the cot and reached under the concealing pillow with both hands to place the cup, then held it there. "Please, press the black button on the remote."

In a hurry to have this over with, he depressed the button. A jolt of electric shock surged through his prostate. Andrea removed the cup and screwed a lid on it, writing his name on the outside of the sample container with a marker.

Disoriented, Cody lay down, keeping the pillow over his traumatized parts. Gasping for air, he started to breathe for the first time in too long. Spots floated before his vision.

"Please, send this to the lab with a rush on the results." Andrea wheeled the cart out of the room to Holden.

"I'm not supposed to leave you alone with him." Holden glanced at Cody.

"He isn't a threat to anyone right now." She pulled the cell door shut.

Cody listened as the locking mechanism engaged, but even if it hadn't, his whole body had succumbed to mild paralysis. What would have happened if he'd pressed the green button on the remote instead? Andrea came to his bedside and sat on the stool, taking his hand in hers. He didn't fight her because he couldn't.

"Lisa wants children." He did too, though having them frightened him because of what the government might do to them.

"You should rest, Cody." She massaged his hand in a soothing manner with both of hers. "Lisa loves you. We will find a cure for Rotcargathogen. And then we will rescue her from your brother. You have nothing to worry about, especially if you're sterile. It means you won't be in the breeding program anymore. You'll be free."

"Have you–" Cody struggled to speak the words. "Have you used this remote control before?"

"Yes." Andrea's hands stilled. "You and I are matched."

"What?" Cody jerked his hand away, adding two plus two together to reveal the foursome. "Lisa and I will never comply with the Matchmaker's plans."

"Lisa doesn't have a choice, and neither do we." Andrea stared at her hands in her lap. "If you're sterile, then she'll be given to someone else."

"I'll never forgive myself if that happens." Cody growled at the injustice of this treatment, staring at the ceiling in an effort to calm himself.

"Your medical chart says you had the fever when you were young." Andrea pocketed the remote control. "It isn't your fault."

"Holden isn't from EIGHT." Cody searched her expression for clues. "He never had the plague."

"Correct." Andrea met his gaze. "But the Matchmaker doesn't want him to reproduce."

"What do you mean?" Cody's sluggish mind wrestled with the idea. "Are you saying that Holden was sterilized by the Matchmaker?"

"Soon after his birth." Andrea nodded. "His parentage was unsanctioned."

Nausea assailed Cody's stomach. How long had this breeding program been in effect? How many generations had been manipulated? When would it end?

"Could you and Lisa both be pregnant with my children?" Cody hugged the pillow and curled into the fetal position, facing Andrea.

"Maybe." Andrea's eyes overflowed with tears. "Can you imagine what she must be going through with your brother right now? He's a monster for raping her."

"Are you sure he's infected her?" Cody's innate scepticism kept him from accepting things at face value.

"That's what I was told." Andrea sobbed for a while and then wiped her nose with a cloth from her pocket. "He infected the Matchmaker as well. So, our resources to find the cure are ensured."

Cody laughed bitterly. "That's why they told you Lisa was infected. They know we love her and will do everything we can to save her. The Matchmaker is counting on it, not because he cares about Lisa, but to save himself." Cody had met Praetorius, and his brother was fighting for justice. "What if Praetorius hasn't infected Lisa at all?"

"He's a rogue executioner capable of anything." Andrea stood.

"Yes." Cody grabbed the remote from her pocket and threw it to smash against the wall. "That's what he has to be in a society like ours."

Chapter Ten

Lisa and Royce crossed terrain unlike anything she had encountered. The ripple-track rover crunched over loose volcanic rocks. Dark in color, the undulating landscape opened up in a gaping hole ahead of them.

Royce parked the rover in a sparse patch of red sand, laying the solar panels down to absorb power from the last rays of direct sunlight. Gathering the things he'd stolen from NINE, the two of them hiked into the enormous opening in the ground. She descended with him into a lava tube of gigantic proportions.

Eventually, he led her along a side tunnel. At a hatch in the wall, they cycled through the airlock and decontamination rinse to enter a locker room. Royce pried loose the latches on his suit to remove his helmet and gauntlets. His chest heaved as he took a deep breath and set down the stolen items.

Lisa unsealed as well, straightening her glasses on her nose. The fresh air inside the room reassured her that life was worth living. Shivering with cold, she panted for breath, thankful to be free of the claustrophobic environmental suit.

She needed water and to use the facilities, but she waited for him to act first. Her small stature and lack of fighting skills left her at his mercy. After losing his mother, she had no desire to upset him further, especially when she suspected that he had figured out it was her fault.

"A life needs saved." Royce opened a locker and tossed her a container of liquid. "Are you willing to make a sacrifice?" His deep voice rasped.

"Yes." Lisa felt obligated since she needed his help to rescue Cody. "I'd like to save as many lives as possible."

"Let's start with one." Royce rummaged through the Matchmaker's medical kit to produce a packet of sample medications, ripping a capsule from its packaging and handing it to her. "Take this."

The intensity of his strained expression gave her pause. Regardless, she swallowed the medication with the entire contents of the bottle. Trembling with relief at the needed hydration, she sat on a bench to await the effects of the drug.

"I didn't expect you to do it." He drank electrolytes as he watched her closely.

"You don't know me." She had devoted her life to improving the situation of others. "Or maybe you do." He had spoken in Korean and could be the one who had translated her innermost thoughts and prayers to their mutual enemy.

"You're not the criminal I believed you to be." He veiled his gaze with long, dark eyelashes. "But I can't tell if you're the girl I thought I knew or not." He shook his head. "Anyway, thank you for telling me about how my friends died."

"I hope it helped you find closure." She walked over to the sink and refilled the bottle.

"Shade and Alik were trying to rescue Cody." Royce took a deep breath and let it out slowly. "She had asked me to let them know if I ever saw him."

"I had no idea." Lisa clasped her trembling hands around the bottle to steady them. "Why would she do that?"

"She loved him." Royce shrugged. "I guess they grew up together."

"I don't understand." Lisa frowned in confusion. "He never spoke of anyone named Shade–" Lisa's hand flew to cover her mouth, sticking in the blood of the Matchmaker's henchmen that coated her skin from when Royce had killed them two days ago. "His shade tree mechanic?"

"That's right." Royce guided her by the hand and the small of the back to sit on the bench and sat beside her. "It's the name she chose after Alik freed us from the dungeon."

"I killed Cody's Erica?" Lisa tried to slow her heavy breathing. "He told me she died when they were in high school."

"She never told me her real name." Royce folded his hands in his lap. "The government often fakes people's deaths when they want to use them for something secret."

"No." Lisa's blood rushed in her ears. "It can't be Erica. What did she look like?"

"She was beautiful, tall, blonde, and had large breasts." Royce frowned. "I can't blame Alik for falling in love with her."

Lisa stared at his bitter expression in shock. "The description matches. I killed the love of Cody's life. How will he ever forgive me?"

"Why does that matter?" Royce met her gaze. "You won't be seeing him again anyway. Nobody returns from the Incursion Zone." He worked his torso out the neck hole of his environmental suit. "You should use the facilities first, unless you want me to contaminate you with the rot."

"I–" Lisa's hands flailed despite her efforts to control them. "Well–" She struggled to catch her breath. "I'll hurry." She reluctantly worked her shoulders and arms out of the suit, but hesitated to expose her breasts.

"I've seen everything you have." He eyed her erratic breathing with a critical gaze. "Modesty between us is irrelevant at this point."

She'd seen him naked too when he'd changed into his suit back in NINE. But she had no desire to see the sores on his oddly hairless groin for a second time. With no other option, however, she shimmied out of her suit.

He watched her every move. She used the toilet and shower as fast as she could, then covered with a towel. His attention turned to the recharging unit where he plugged in her suit to sanitize the interior, power up the battery, and recycle the air in the cylinder.

As she searched the lockers for extra small clothing, he used the facilities. She dressed in a plain, gray uniform and black boots, wrapping her hair in the towel. The shower turned on just as the recharging unit sounded its completion. Without looking at him, she detached her suit, started his, and collapsed hers for ease of carrying.

"You surprise me." He gingerly dried the wounds on his most intimate place.

She hadn't meant to look. "How so?" She glanced anywhere but at his spreading sores.

"I thought you'd be more curious." He strode over to stand next to her.

"How long do you have to live?" Following Cody's advice to stand up to bullies, she faced the brutal killer with boldness.

"That's not what I expected you to ask, but I'll answer." He wrapped the towel around his waist. "I'll be dead within a matter of days."

"Do you think some kind of natural remedy might help?" She had seen the benefits of herbs and teas before. "Vinegar and honey, maybe? Really, I can't let you die without trying to help."

"I thought you hated me." His upper body flexed with tension.

"What?" She stared at his rippling muscles. "I need your help to save Cody from the Matchmaker because I'm stuck underground until I find a way to block the signal to my implant."

"So, you need me." He inserted the towel into the washing machine. "And I need you."

"What?" She scrutinized his flaccid central member in confusion. "Do all men look alike?"

"No." He widened his stance. "I've been told I'm exceptional."

"Oh." She shook her head and met his gaze. "It's strange." A shiver traversed her spine. "Other than your lack of body hair, you look like Cody."

"Exactly alike?" He held her gaze.

"Almost." She shuddered. "It's disturbing."

"My appearance should disturb you, Neesa." He scowled. "The dungeon keeper prevents facial and body hair development to preserve the youthful appearance of the sex slaves for as long as possible." He clenched his jaw. "Because certain elites prefer children."

"Children?" Agape, her knees wobbled. "Who would do that?" She planned to report them, though that was stupid since they were above the law. "I want names."

"You never did." He walked over and opened a locker. "That's all that matters at the moment."

"I had no idea such things took place in the colonies." Shaking violently, she sat on the bench. "It's illegal. Slavery and sexual abuse are crimes. How can this happen?"

"The elites do whatever they want." His hairless chest heaved with a heavy breath. "The outposts have secret dungeons." He dressed in white underclothes. "Since you were a virgin until two days ago, I'm guessing you never visited them. But you're the only member of the Gold Circle who hasn't."

"I'm not–" Lisa's jaw dropped. "I'm not a party to organized crime."

"You say that." He laughed darkly. "Maybe you believe it, but they've been using you since you could talk."

The blood drained from her face and neck until her hands chilled. "I pray that's not true." If it was, then her gifts and abilities had done as much harm as good.

"You're not lying about that." He stared at the floor. "But how do I know you didn't sell out? I was sure you had when I didn't find your name on the petition to stop the Gold Council from executing Shim's Resource Transfer Protocol. I thought that meant you were guilty." His hands flexed and a dark look entered his brown eyes. "That's why I strangled you in the hospital."

"Oh." She had no memory of the assassination attempt. "Cody suspected the same thing." She grew faint, remembering his cold accusations. "But, I destroyed my protocol so that it couldn't be abused. I had no idea what the council was doing. That's why my name wasn't on the petition. Though, it sounds like the other directors knew what was going on, including my best friend Andrea. Does that mean that she's part of the Gold Circle?" Her friend's betrayal wounded her deeply.

"Yes." He nodded, dressing in a gray uniform. "Andrea Tran's signature was there." Royce's Adam's apple bobbed in his throat. "I thought you'd betrayed everything you believed in. It was as if it had never been true, and that God didn't exist. It destroyed me." His eyes took on a deeply stricken look.

"Royce, do you share my faith?" She struggled to understand his torment.

"Yes." He turned away. "I believed the Scriptures your family read and the prayers you offered, but I was a fool for thinking someone like me had a chance at redemption." His hands balled into fists. "Now there's no way I can face God with clean hands."

"Though thy sins be as scarlet, they shall be as white as snow." Lisa's heart beat faster. "Repentance is possible."

"How?" He shook his head. "Not even God can love me after what I've done. I tried to kill you, and you weren't even the Shim responsible. Sahra betrayed the principles your family teaches, but I've heard her prayers too. She questions everything, so her faithlessness isn't a surprise. You trusted her completely, though, and that gave her access to your work. She's the one to blame for this."

"Sahra wouldn't do that." Lisa didn't want to suspect her sister. "But she may have sacrificed her integrity for the sake of our family. I've been agonizing over it for days. Her going from SEVEN to TEN, even for a temporary assignment, is an incredible jump in status. It may have been a reward. I just don't want to believe she'd betray me. I love my sister. We're simpatico." It was a line from an old movie that she and Sahra had watched as children more times than she could count.

"That's the trouble with angels." He pulled on a pair of boots and laced them.

"How do you know so much about my family?" She stared at his severe expression.

"I pulled double-duty as an interpreter." He met her gaze.

"Then you know everything about me." Lisa's heart thudded erratically in her chest. "And because of you, my enemies were able to manipulate me." Her hands clenched into fists as she stood to face him.

"Alik rescued me from our enemies eleven months ago." Royce squared his shoulders. "Think about that, Shim Neesa." He spoke in Korean.

Stillness overtook her. She'd been safe while he was listening. Only when someone else took over his duties had everything started going wrong.

Sahra had betrayed her. The pain of that truth sank deep into Lisa's chest. Who else had she misjudged?

The man in the locker room with her came to mind. Furious at the whole universe, she dismissed the notion as ludicrous. Royce Nedge would try to kill her again the moment she opposed him, and that meant that her escape plan had to be perfect.

Chapter Eleven

Cody dressed in a red uniform without insignia and waited for Andrea to return from the laboratory. When she returned, he followed her from his prison cell. Holden brought up the rear, armed with a stun pistol on his belt.

"When will the lab have the test results completed?" Cody asked.

"Outpost labs aren't great." Holden answered as they headed for the docking portals.

"True." Andrea glanced over her shoulder. "That's why I flash froze half of the sample to take with us." She held up a metal cylinder. "The rest is being imaged under a microscope for analysis. The medical technician will send me the data."

"Oh." Cody could feel his pulse against his eardrums to the rhythm of his distress. "I just wish I had the answer already."

"Well–" Andrea glanced at him again. "I was curious too. So, I took a look through the microscope before I left the lab. The slide had very few sperm, but they were motile."

"Motility is good." Cody's chest heaved with relief and dread at the same time. "So, I could still become a father?"

"Maybe." Andrea shook her head. "The results are not definitive. But at least, you are not sterile. There may be a way to increase your sperm production. So, there's hope."

"Increase it, how?" Cody didn't like the sound of that.

"Nutrition, including an increase in protein." Andrea avoided his gaze as they boarded the rover. "And a more natural approach to coupling with less frequency than the Matchmaker had planned might help."

"Now, wait just a—" Cody started to say.

"Relax." Holden shoved Cody into a passenger seat.

"Don't worry." Andrea took a seat across the aisle from him. "My ovulation cycle just ended, and we don't know what the results of the tests will reveal, so it will be weeks before we have to concern ourselves with a strategy."

"I won't accept you, Andrea." Cody buckled his five-point harness. "Taking samples the way you do amounts to sexual assault."

"I agree." Andrea's tone elevated. "But haven't you considered that the process is assault for me too?"

"And me." Holden sat in the pilot's seat. "Well, emotionally anyway. Andrea and I had just figured out a system that worked for both of us. Now, here you come, giving her what she needs when I can't. It's not right."

"I'm not going to do it, Holden." Cody's cheeks flooded with heat. "I love Lisa. I want children with her and no one else."

"Please." Andrea looked at Holden in the rearview mirror. "We must be on our way."

"Fine." Holden released the rover from the docking hatch and accelerated along the spur road, departing through the briefly open gate of the perimeter fence to merge onto the Glass Highway. "But I don't even understand where we're headed, other than north, because TEN is supposed to be east. It doesn't make sense."

"Right." Cody had been thinking the same thing. "Outpost Juliet isn't located in quite the right place." He used his perfect memory to visualize the topographic map of Mars that he had studied in the academy. "We're already too far north, according to these rock formations." He looked closely at the area visible outside the rover.

"Um." Holden leaned to the side, glancing back at Cody. "Take a look at this."

"I see it." Cody's stress level elevated as the computer indicated that a weapon's system had a target lock on their rover. "Best maintain our itinerary." What other choice did they have other than compliance?

Chapter Twelve

Lisa followed Royce out the rear exit from the locker room sure that Sahra must have been protecting the family the same way Lisa had tried to do. He selected 'sanitize the room' on the keypad and secured the door. They stood in a dark tunnel, carrying the gear he'd stolen from NINE.

"It's quite a hike to the facilities chamber." Royce strode into the darkness. "Can your stubby legs keep up with me?"

"My legs aren't stubby." She hustled after him.

"Then it's your asthmatic lungs that are the problem." His footfalls resounded on the steady incline.

She doubled her efforts, annoyed that he knew so much about her. He spoke Korean and had listened in on every private conversation she'd ever had. Even worse, he knew things she only told God.

"I have more stamina than you think." Winded, she bumped into him and recoiled backward.

He grabbed her by the shirt front, preventing her from tumbling down the slope. "Give me your gear."

"I can carry it." She panted so hard she was seeing motes of light in her vision.

"You're wasting time." He snatched her specialized toolkit from her hand and clipped it to one of the rifle straps crisscrossed across his chest. "You made me a promise." He clipped the medical kit he'd been carrying on the other side and carried the environmental suits one under each arm. "Do you plan to keep it, or do I have to administer the legal punishment for deceit?"

"I promised to save a life." She struggled to catch her breath, wondering what he meant. "You didn't say what I needed to do to accomplish the task."

"I'll give you a clue, it involves one of your most attractive features." He chuckled. "Just be glad it isn't me who needs them."

"I don't understand." A shiver of dread traversed her spine. "But, I'll keep my promise."

"Good." His footfalls pressed forward along a strip of glowing lights. "Keep up with me."

"I'm coming." She hurried after him.

"Is that an invitation?" He glanced over his shoulder.

"I won't be any good to you infected." She almost wished she could go back to three days ago when she wouldn't have understood the innuendo.

"I would use protective gear." His voice echoed back to her from the top of a flight of stairs.

"Retaliation won't be necessary." She climbed after him, chewing her bottom lip. "I'll keep my word."

"Better run." His voice had become faint in the distance. "I took the long way here because of that tracker in your head."

"I'm coming." She winced. "I'm right behind you." She amended.

"Some people like that almost as much, but you don't have the equipment for it." His voice echoed back to her.

"I'm sure I can find something in my toolkit." She fumed.

"I'll take that as an invitation." He chuckled.

"No." Furious, she ran faster. "It wasn't a solicitation."

"That's disappointing." Royce's voice traveled from far ahead.

The only man she wanted was Cody. Seeing him again would be enough to make her weep for joy. He would be welcome in her bed, but this degenerate enemy had no right to threaten her with infection.

"Is it much farther." She couldn't catch her breath.

He mumbled something, but he'd put too much distance between them for her to understand his words. Far ahead in a spot of light, he entered a code on a keypad. His boot clapped against the frame of the hatch as he pulled hard.

Air whooshed from the tunnel into the next room. That kind of pressure differential meant a loss of air, and alerted her to danger. Royce opened the hatch wide, taking a bolt of blue light to the chest before he dropped to the concrete floor.

"Drag him inside. Hurry, we're losing time." A wiry man with a flop of dark hair stepped over Royce's body with a stun pistol in hand. "What have we here?" He eyed Lisa.

"I can seal that breach." She faced him, tugging her uniform straight. "I have the tools right there." She pointed at the specialized toolkit next to Royce.

"Good luck finding the hole." The man warily made his way toward her. "The scrapyard is in atmospheric collapse. I'm sorry to say it, but you must stay with your husband. I can't take you from him."

Lisa noted the tone of regret in the man's voice. She obeyed his command to stay with her master and hustled through the hatch, stepping into a cavern brimming with oddly quiet life-support equipment. Royce lay unconscious on the sandstone floor.

"We're going to need your suits and stun rifles." The wiry man counted out fifty-seven tokens into her hand. "That should be enough to compensate." He faced a young man in the cavern. "Will this fit you?"

"I can squeeze into it." The young man spoke to the wiry man. "Look at the bruising. He's been battering her." He pointed at Lisa.

"He has the Rot." The wiry man scowled. "It makes people mean."

"Royce hasn't infected me." Lisa raised her chin. "Both suits have gone through a sanitization cycle. It's safe to use them."

"We can't leave her with him." The young man peered at Lisa.

"We don't have a choice." The wiry man waved the boy into the tunnel. "It's the law, and I have no intention of facing the consequences for breaking up a union." Lingering a moment, he handed Lisa a knife and took back two tokens. "You'll live longer if he's not breathing. Now, tell me where you left your rover."

"Outside the black rock cave entrance." She searched his Latino features. "It's a stealth rover."

"We're covering the tracks of the wrecker crews." He gave her a nod. "I hope you've sealed the leak and are still alive when we return."

The two outlaws departed, sealing and locking the hatch after them. Lisa dropped the knife along with the tokens beside Royce's prone body. Reaching into the toolkit for a heat scanner, she set to work finding the breach. This facility wouldn't fail if an engineer could save it.

Chapter Thirteen

After five hours in the rover at top speed, Cody couldn't believe his eyes. Holden piloted them from the Glass Highway onto a bridge. Ahead lay a structure like the central tube of a colony. Other bridges radiated from it like the spokes of an ancient bicycle wheel to form an enclosure level with the ground.

There were no habitats. Instead, across the expanse between bridges lay a flat lattice work of transparent aluminum. Beneath that lay nothing but white.

This was strange. He couldn't see the bottom. The pit of his stomach dropped as he realize it was a crater.

"This is what they're stealing the air and water for." He leaned as far as he could to see down, but nothing was visible.

"What do you mean?" Holden looked over the side too.

"NINE isn't the only colony in jeopardy." Cody clenched his jaw. "Resources have been repeatedly transferred from all of the colonies. Ask your wife."

"TEN doesn't exist." Andrea met her husband's gaze in the rearview mirror. "Instead, they built something much bigger. I signed a petition to end the transfers, but it was intercepted by outlaws."

"Yes, I lost it in the rover wreck last month." Cody scowled at her. "My brother showed it to me after he broke into my apartment and overpowered me four days ago." He pointed at the clouds under the latticework. "By my estimation, this is Gail Crater and that's water vapor."

"But..." Andrea stared across the covered expanse. "It's enormous."

Holden piloted the rover slowly, looking at everything with wide eyes. At the central tube, he made an arc and backed up to a docking ring. The rover sealed and he opened the hatches.

"The air smells different here." Holden inhaled a deeper breath. "I like it."

"You're right." Andrea followed him. "It's fresh like a fruit tree or something."

Cody followed them from the docking ring to the promenade surprised that they hadn't been greeted by armed guards. The signature trees of every colony filled the shady space beneath a high latticework. Between polished, golden colored concrete walkways, grassy areas bordered by park benches filled the space while stores and restaurants comprised the perimeter.

"Where are all the people?" Cody wondered out loud.

"There's a clerk in that clothing store." Andrea pointed through the front window at a woman dressing a manakin in lingerie.

Cody looked away, thinking of Lisa on their wedding day when they'd stopped at EIGHT and she'd taken him shopping. She didn't realize it, but he'd seen her pick out a white, lace neglige. Then, after the wreck, he'd nearly died catching a glimpse of her in it as she changed into an environmental suit.

Admittedly, he'd enjoyed the view of her without it even more. Until he'd passed out from lack of oxygen, that is. He shook his head to clear it of the memory of her angelic curves bathed in starlight.

"Hey." Holden waved a hand in front of Cody's face. "We're overdue at the laboratory. Let's go."

Andrea had already walked far ahead of them. Cody nodded, putting away the image of the woman he loved for later recall. His wife may actually need him to find a cure. His brother did for sure. However, it galled him to help the Matchmaker.

Taking everything in along the way, Cody followed Andrea to the lab. A large team of scientists bustled around state of the art equipment, seeking a cure for the Rot. Cody picked up a data pad on a counter, reading through a brief on the disease and the researchers' progress toward finding a cure.

Rage swelled in his chest. They were using human test subjects, including children. Though, as he read further, he realized that they weren't infecting them just trying experimental treatments on people who were already sick.

Since carriers of the Rot had been euthenized immediately after diagnosis in the past, this was a step in the right direction. Well, it would be if the patients had signed a consent form for the experimental treatments. However, no such documents were included in the report.

Cody inhaled an expansive breath and let it out slowly as he scrolled to the bottom of the findings. Andrea skimmed the report before making eye contact. A frown creased her brow.

"They haven't found anything hopeful." Cody walked over to her.

"Eliminating possible treatments is helpful." Her frown deepened.

"Yes, making sure that no known medication has any beneficial effect is just great." Cody scoffed and shook his head. "This leaves us with what? Home remedies?"

Andrea's eyebrows lifted. "Ancient, herbal remedies are a possibility." She shook her head. "No, we'll just have to rely on chemistry." She looked him in the eyes. "Study. Meditate. Do what you do better than anyone else, and I'll consult with the experts on the team." She strode toward a clutch of her research and development colleagues in white lab coats.

Cody wandered to a quiet corner of the room, found an armchair, and did exactly as she'd said. Except that he focused his research on herbal cures for skin diseases. If no one else was going to utilize ancient wisdom, then he would have to find a natural cure.

Chapter Fourteen

A chill seeped into Royce's painful existence, compounding his misery. The unforgiving concrete lay at his back, or he lay on it, he couldn't tell at first. Exercising the use of his right hand, he found the cause of his headache.

A large lump had formed on the back of his head. Someone from the scrapyard crew had stunned him the instant he'd opened the hatch to the facilities chamber. Furious, he climbed to his feet.

Flaco's knife lay on the floor amidst an embarrassingly large pile of tokens. Royce gathered them up, filling his pockets. Then, he tucked the knife in his waistband.

Surveying the silent facilities chamber, he spotted Lisa's petite form crouched by the far exterior airlock. She had her back to him. What was she busy doing?

As he stalked toward her, she twisted the cap onto a tube of sealant and scanned the patch job with an electronic device from her toolkit. What had she sold for all this money? The stun rifles and environmental suits were missing.

Where was Shade's baby? Flaco wouldn't have taken him if he was desperate enough for environmental suits to take them by force. Grief hit Royce square in the chest.

"Where's the boy?" Bitterness soured his stomach.

"The young man went with the wiry man." Lisa stood to face him, dropping the tube into her toolkit with a smile. "I've sealed the breach."

"I brought you here to save his life." Royce menaced over her, incensed by her nonchalant response.

"He looked fine." She took a step backward. "They can safely return just as soon as I fix the life support equipment."

"He's starving to death." Royce clapped his hands on her slight shoulders and pressed her against the hatch.

"I don't have any food." Her brows drew together.

"You are the food." He palmed her small breast. "You were supposed to nurse him. Why would Flaco take him?"

"I don't understand." She pried his hand from her chest. "Are you talking about a baby?"

"Yes." He pressed his body against hers, pinning her to the hatch. "Where's the boy?"

"I haven't seen a baby." Her chest heaved as she hyperventilated.

"They didn't take him?" He held her gaze.

"Not a baby, but there was an adolescent boy with the wiry man." She tried to shove him away. "Please, let me save our lives."

"No baby?" Royce shook from head to toe in disbelief, taking a step back. "Were we too late?" He looked toward the reclamation unit. "Is he with his mother then?"

"Did his mother die?" Lisa glanced from Royce to the reclamation unit and back. "You brought me here to nurse a motherless infant?"

"To make amends." Royce collapsed onto his backside on the floor.

"Amends?" Lisa sank to her knees. "Who was his mother?"

"Shade." He rocked in distress.

"The baby died?" Lisa's voice held torment. "Because of me?"

"He needed milk to survive." Royce drew her onto his lap.

"God forgive me." She took his hands in hers.

"Why do you need mercy?" He held her gaze in anguish.

"I killed Erica and her baby." Tears spilled from Lisa's eyes.

"It was an accident." He pulled her closer, pressing his face into her hair.

"Their deaths are my fault." She shuddered.

"I forgive you." Seeking solace, he kissed her forehead, cheek, and lips.

She bucked hard. "I'm a married woman."

"Yes, Neesa." He held her tenderly. "That's what I've been trying to explain. I'm your husband under the laws of the Northern Territory. And Shade's baby is not the only child in need of a mother."

"But, I love Cody." She planted her hands in the center of his chest and pushed.

"He's already been matched with other women." Royce regretted having to tell her this.

"Cody would never do that." She shoved even harder.

"He has no choice." Emotion choked Royce. "All of those women are probably pregnant, Neesa." He glanced at her abdomen. "Just like you."

"Pregnant?" Lisa stilled.

"Probably." He closed his eyes. "It's how the breeding program works, but I can't face God without doing everything I can to protect my children, Neesa. That's why I need you to inherit my holdings when I die."

"I don't understand." She frowned.

"Marry me." He averted his gaze. "It's not what you think. I'm not asking for your love. I nearly killed you." His hopes for redemption resided in her hands. "I know you must hate me, but I'm willing to make up for the pain I've caused you by providing you with pleasure if that's what you want."

"What?" Her head shook. "You can't trade sex for my forgiveness. Love isn't to be bought and sold. It is a gift. I gave my gift to Cody. I cannot give myself to you."

"But the law says you can." He pleaded with her. "And I desperately need you to agree to be my wife."

"The laws of men mean less to me than the dictates of my conscience." Her chest rose with a deep breath. "When I meet God, I want to do it with a pure heart. I'm not sure how to forgive you for what you've done, but holding bitterness inside me is painful. So, I'd like to pray about it."

"Go ahead." He closed his eyes.

She clasped her hands as she voiced a soft-spoken prayer. He listened as she wrestled with God over the suffering he'd caused her loved ones to endure while she languished in a coma. She poured out her heart to her Father in Heaven and found a way out of her grief to a place of compassion.

He marveled at the grace that she received and extended to him. Wrapping his arms around her, he exercised faith to accept the Atonement of Jesus Christ. In that moment, peace entered his soul, filling him with a warm light.

Into the silence, the whimper of an infant echoed in the chamber. At first he didn't comprehend it. Fortunately, the sound repeated, causing him to look toward a pile of rags that rustled with movement in a corner.

"They left him." Relief washed over Royce like a warm shower, and he raised his bowed head to meet Lisa's gaze. "There's still a chance for you to save him."

"Do you have something to induce lactation?" Lisa looked at the baby's tiny waving fists.

"I already gave it to you." Royce released her, despite his need for her warmth and the comfort her closeness.

"Why would they leave a child behind to die?" She met his gaze.

"I guess they had to." Royce helped her to stand. "He's too young to take out in an environmental suit, even if they had an extra one."

"I don't understand." Lisa strode toward the pile of rags and carefully lifted the weakly mewling infant from among them. "He looks like you." Cradling the baby in her arms, she soothed his cries with soft-spoken words.

"He's not mine." Royce rubbed his face with his trembling hands.

"Is he starving?" Lisa caressed the baby's cheek, and he suckled the air.

"We feed him what we have." Royce struggled to keep his emotions out of his voice. "But he needs mother's milk. Will you accept him?"

"Yes." Lisa stared at the infant's face. "When will my milk come in?"

A lump formed in Royce's throat, preventing him from a response. She faced him, making eye contact. He regained control of his emotions and closed the distance between them.

"All you need to do is nurse him." He stilled his shaking hands behind his back. "He will bring your milk in."

"You brought me here for Shade's baby?" Lisa held his gaze.

"Yes." Royce choked on his emotions.

"Thank you." Tears filled her eyes. "I'm grateful for the chance to make amends in some small way." She sat cross legged on the floor, cradling the baby in her lap. "I've never done this before."

"Willingness is all that matters." Royce let out a tremulous breath as he sat in front of her. "The boy knows what to do."

She unbuttoned her uniform top, guiding the infant to her breast. The baby latched on and suckled. Lisa winced, but made no complaint. All the while, Royce watched in wonderment at her tenderness because this was the selfless Lisa Shim he'd always hoped to meet.

Chapter Fifteen

Lisa had seen her mother nurse her seven younger siblings. Sitting across from Royce with the infant at her breast, she hoped there was something there to nourish the baby. The discomfort of his suckling was worth enduring if it saved his life.

"How old is he?" She tried to distract Royce from staring at her chest by engaging him in conversation.

"Six months." Royce scooted closer, his gaze unwavering from her breast.

"How long has he been without infant formula?" She winced as the baby's suckling strengthened.

"A week." Royce stroked the boy's brown hair.

"Where did you find formula in a place like this?" She looked around the cluttered chamber at the broken equipment scavenged from a variety of rovers.

"I traded sex in NINE." Royce's stricken gaze lowered to the hands he'd folded in his lap.

"Infant formula is rationed." The baby whimpered fitfully at her lack of milk, but Lisa gathered her courage and changed him to the other side. "Who would give you any when it meant their child would go hungry?"

"The kind of people with Rotcargathogen." Royce met her gaze. "That's where I caught the Rot."

"You became infected in NINE?" Lisa grabbed the baby's free hand as he scratched her breast with tiny fingernails in need of clipping.

With the increased leverage of a handhold, the boy hungrily rooted against her breast, making her sore. Royce grimaced. She hadn't expected sympathy from him.

"Does it hurt?" She wanted to change the subject.

He nodded, staring with wide eyes. "It sure looks like it does."

"Not me." She suffered through it because the baby needed her. "I was asking about your illness."

"Yes." He raised his gaze from the feeding child. "But I wasn't expecting to survive long enough for it to become this painful." He adjusted his position and sat cross legged. "I sent everything I traded for back here with Flaco three weeks ago. Then, I set out to execute you. I had to do more trade to stay hidden. I'm not sure who infected me. By that point, I didn't care. NINE is a cesspool. It was only a matter of time."

"You risked your life for your son." Lisa frowned as she focused on the baby again in confusion. "That makes you a good father. Maybe if you'd gone back with Flaco, then you wouldn't have become sick."

"Cegory Eden isn't my son." Royce's hands gripped his knees. "He isn't even Shade's biological baby. She was a surrogate slave for your cousin and his wife. My guess is that he's theirs."

"My cousin?" Lisa searched Royce's expression for an explanation.

"Councilor Han didn't want his wife to lose her figure." Royce's expression darkened. "Plus, he enjoyed a rough ride now and then at Shade's expense. His wife liked to watch. So, when Alik rescued me, I bargained to save Shade as well. Not many men would have dared to take a pregnant surrogate from an outpost dungeon, but Alik did. It helped that she could pilot a rover, and I'm a quick learner. With false credentials from my mother, we stole three, state of the art, laser deflection tanks, and caravanned them straight into the Northern Territories without anyone raising a single question. Alik traded them to the revolutionaries for the scrapyard."

"He sounds like a good man." She pondered on the kind of courage it must have taken to break into an outpost and steal slaves. "I'm sorry he died the way he did. I'm ashamed of Councilor Han. I've never met him or his wife because he disowned my father for marrying my mother against his advice." She glanced at Royce to see if he held the shameful situation against her. "She timed out in protest of the marriage mandate, and father saved her from execution."

"And you saved Cody after he timed out." Royce raised his gaze from the hands he'd meshed together in his lap. "That's why I believed he was a slave. I never would have guessed he'd go to that length to capture a criminal."

Lisa gasped as baby Cegory detached from her breast. "Cody eventually told me all that he could." She covered her chest and raised the boy to her shoulder, patting his little back.

"Why didn't he tell you who his mother was?" Royce captured her gaze.

"It was a difficult subject." Lisa stared, wondering what he meant by using the past tense. "He didn't like to talk about her?"

"There's a lot you don't know." Royce looked away.

"So it would seem." Lisa buttoned her top with one hand. "I'll ask Cody about it after we rescue him."

The baby burped. She cradled him in her arms and watched him fall asleep. In that moment, an intense feeling of love swelled inside her chest.

"Thank you for bringing me here." She snuggled the baby close, smiling as she glanced at Royce. "I never expected this kind of attachment to sweep over me so quickly."

His expressive brown eyes captured her attention. She recognized something in them that she'd only seen from Cody. Confused, she looked away.

"Neither did I, especially after how much I've hated you for the past month." He shook his head.

"What are you saying?" She watched his face for evidence.

"It's hard to explain." He grabbed the pile of rags, sorting through them to arrange a makeshift bed. "I used to listen to the recordings of your gentle laughter, soft-spoken conversations, and earnest prayers, committing every nuance of your inflection to memory and remembering those moments in times of distress to escape from what was happening to me. You saved me when no one else had that power."

"What happened to you, Royce?" She wasn't sure she wanted to know the answer, but since it was happening to Cody now, she had to know.

"Buyers came for me from the time I was born." He swallowed, causing his Adam's apple to rise and fall. "At first, I cried. Then I fought. And when I could talk, I begged them to stop. My mother found me as a toddler and taught me what she did when bad things happened. After that, I went somewhere else in my mind."

"What does that mean?" She hoped Cody could do the same thing to escape his torture.

"I let my body go limp, thinking about something else so I didn't have to feel anything they did to me." He fidgeted with his hands. "If I had fought them, then they would have drugged me into behaving like a sex crazed animal."

"How do you know that?" She dreaded the answer.

"Because once in a while buyers requested the treatment." He stared at his hands in his lap. "Those men always regretted it afterward, I think."

"I don't understand." Dread filled her with apprehension.

"It's hazy in my mind, frenzied, erotic." His brows lowered. "There was blood all over me the last time when I came out of it alone on the bed." He glanced at her. "I never saw that man again."

"Did you kill him?" She hardly dared to ask.

"I don't know." He stared as if into a blank memory. "But the overseer never used those drugs on me again. He just let me lay still for buyers after that. When it came time to impregnate women, he used the stimulator."

"What's that?" She shuddered to think of it.

"It's an implant that does the work for me." He climbed to his feet and went to the medical kit, pulling out the locket. "There are buttons inside this device that control my body. Press the green one and you can ride me as long as you like. Press the black one and it's over with in a few seconds. The women chose the way they wanted to do it. I just lay there wishing I were in your family's apartment having Sunday dinner with you. Or I'd pretend we were in your lab creating the things you dream of at night. Only once in a while did I imagine what it would be like to give you a child. I knew you'd be a good mother, and I hoped the other women would be too. If they enjoyed their time with me, then maybe they wouldn't resent their baby and treat the child badly."

"Why would they do that?" Lisa struggled to comprehend the things he said, but none of it confused her more than this.

"Because." His watery gaze captured hers. "The government forced them to have a third or forth child after their husbands died. They didn't want to be with me any more than I wanted them. They weren't buyers in the same way as the others. They were compelled under penalty of death. Many of them wept the whole time."

Lisa covered her mouth in distress, wishing she could do something to stop this kind of abuse. But she was helpless. She hadn't even known about it, and now Cody was suffering the same treatment that Royce had endured.

"I'm sorry you went through this." Large tears rolled from her eyes when she blinked. "Have you ever checked on your children?" She looked away, wiping her cheeks. "I mean, are they all right?"

"I found one of the mother's about ten months ago." Royce dropped the locket back into the kit and came over to sit on the makeshift bed. "My daughter looked healthy and happy, playing with her three older brothers at the park on the promenade in TWO. The woman took photos of the children building sand castles. She pushed our little girl in a toddler seat on the swing set. They ate a picnic lunch. Then the woman saw me and the color drained from her face, so I walked away. I wish all of the children were equally loved. I go a little crazy when I find they're being abused. The boy with Flaco is one of them."

"You rescued him?" Lisa kissed the sleeping baby's brow and laid him on the bed next to his father. "You're a better man than I imagined."

"Having the children safe helps assuage my guilt." Royce unlaced his boots and took them off.

"Why do you feel responsible? You didn't do anything wrong." She couldn't fathom any possible way that he might be culpable given the horrifying circumstances involved.

"I'm their father." He held her gaze. "They need me to protect them."

"How many children do you have?" She asked out of morbid curiosity.

"Two-hundred and ninety-one, I think." His eyelids drooped.

"Incredible." She shook her head. "I had no idea there were so many widows in the colonies."

"Most of them aren't actually widowed." He laid down beside the baby. "The Matchmaker took a lot of men into bondage to work in the second and third crawlers."

"But–" Lisa couldn't believe her ears. "We only have one crawler."

"It's a big secret, but my mother knew." He yawned. "She was the head of the resistance."

"Councilor Albright stood in opposition to the Matchmaker?" This was the first time she'd heard of an active resistance in the colonies.

"Of course, she did. He abused her too." Royce closed his eyes.

"I didn't know?" Lisa's heart pounded in her chest. "She always seemed so powerful."

"Lisa, lay down and rest." He patted the blanket on the other side of the baby.

"I have work to do." She looked longingly at the sleeping place.

"You're safe with me." He held her gaze.

"What do you mean?" She eyed him suspiciously.

"You're the only one I've ever wanted." He sighed. "I know you have deeply rooted needs for intimacy. And as your husband, I'd be honored to fulfill them."

"I need Cody." Lisa climbed to her feet and turned to walk away.

"I am the man of your dreams, Neesa." Royce's voice was heavy with sleep.

"You listened to everything, didn't you?" She stared at his relaxed features as a startling sense of confirmation rang true in her heart. "Regardless, certain intimacies are out of the question. Though, an occasional embrace is acceptable between friends."

"I look forward to holding you." His breathing became steady and slow.

She hadn't thought of it that way. Why had she encouraged him? She headed for her toolkit, seeking comfort in problems solvable with tools and knowhow.

Chapter Sixteen

Cody, Andrea, and Holden descended an elevator to a sub-level luxury apartment that had been intended for his mother. The couple took a spare bedroom. Upon closer inspection of the place, Cody discovered that his mother had prepared a spacious bedroom suite for him.

He pulled underclothes and pajamas from a dresser, heading straight for the shower. The hot water soothed some of the unpleasant feelings that haunted him. The sensations were almost a memory, but not quite.

After the incident in the outpost prison cell, he knew he'd been exploited. His body had been implanted with a device that controlled his most intimate bodily function. A remote control now dictated his physiological response.

Furthermore, whoever held that remote wielded the power to capture his genetic material against his will. He dressed for bed. The only thing saving him from more humiliation was his low sperm count.

He'd never considered that he might have trouble fathering children. He'd harbored qualms about having them because he worried for their safety and agonized over the way they might be used to manipulate him. But, he'd never considered the possibility that he couldn't have them.

The thought that his wife could be forced to reproduce with someone else unmanned him, hollowing out his chest until his shoulders curled forward. When his forehead touched the bathroom mirror, he let the cool surface draw away some of the heat of his shame. His strength, vitality, and capacity had convinced him that he was virile, but maybe he wasn't.

He wished he could talk to Lisa about it. He wished his mother was still alive. She would have ordered humane treatments.

He would have accepted her help. But without Lisa and his mother's aide, only the Matchmaker had the power to alter the stark reality he faced. The urge to vomit assailed him.

Dry heaving, he splashed his face with cool water at the bathroom sink. Breathing heavily, he dried with a hand towel. There must be another option than the foursome with Andrea and Holden.

At least, he had not been compelled to have sex with Andrea. Of course, that was the last thing she and Holden wanted either. So, the knowledge comforted him somewhat as he brushed his teeth with mint flavored toothpaste.

Had he been consulted, he might have consented to the couple using his genetic material to create a family. Except that their morals were askew. Worse yet, it looked like Andrea belonged to the Gold Circle along with all the other directors who had signed the petition.

He wiped out the sink with a wash cloth and hung it to dry. Her corruption alone would have forced him to say no to helping them procreate. Children deserved righteous parents in a committed relationship of love, and he wasn't convinced that Andrea and Holden met that description despite their compliance with the law.

Yet, now he'd been forced to give them what they needed. So, he could one day be the biological father of a baby he hadn't chosen to bring into this world. A relationship of trust with the parents would be the only way he could aide his child.

Nauseous, he walked from the bathroom to the large bed, falling into it exhausted. Tired as he was, however, he crawled out of bed again to kneel in prayer. He'd almost forgotten to pour out his sorrows to his Father in Heaven.

Losing his mother, his wife, and his dignity could have made him bitter. But to his surprise his heart longed for the solace that only the Savior offered. He spent hours working out his problems with the Lord, trying to find his place in all of this and the role he should play in bringing about justice.

He ran Lisa's message to him through his mind interpreting her lip movements. She'd said she loved him and to stay safe. At the end, she'd included a warning that the Matchmaker's name was Albert Albright.

His heart weighed heavily in his chest because he hadn't told her that Addison Albright was his mother. Of course, Addison hadn't told him that his grandfather was the Matchmaker and leading an illegal breeding experiment until right before she'd sedated and abducted him. The shame of it blazoned heat up his neck to blossom in his cheeks.

His one consolation was that his brother had punished the Matchmaker severely. Though, it would have been better for everyone if he'd killed the predator. As it stood, the villain had survived the encounter and ordered Addison's execution.

Albert had killed his daughter, yet he'd spared Lisa. Both women had the neural mesh implant with the same vulnerability. Why would he let Praetorius have Lisa?

It had to have been deliberate. How did Praetorius fit into all of this? Cody sighed, left without a clear answer as he climbed into bed and fell asleep beneath the warm covers only to dream of Andrea Tran.

Chapter Seventeen

Yawning with fatigue, Lisa finished her sweep of the debris-strewn chamber for leaks. She detected none and headed for the huge, ovular, cylinder that was the reclamation unit. Heat radiated from the thick metal.

She sighed in relief. The chemical processes of decomposition were working. Next to the reclamation unit were a dozen steel tanks.

The gages on all but the last one read full pressure. The reclamation unit was effectively collecting methane. That was hazardous if the gas wasn't being used fast enough, but it was a good problem to have because at least the generators had fuel.

She checked each of the machines, only one of them cycled on and off at regular intervals to charge the battery banks, but it was working. The other generators lay in pieces. Someone had tried to repair them without success and left a chaotic mess.

She'd sort that out later. For now, the batteries held a full charge. So, there was plenty of power available.

Why wasn't there much of a draw? Lisa traced the electrical cables fastened along the walls of the roughhewn cavern to various pieces of silent equipment. Finally, she followed a large one to a wall with an airlock in it.

Through the windows in the hatches, she discovered an enormous hydroponics bay. Of the three rows of lights, only a single lamp in the center gave illumination. Plants on the dark edges of the chamber had turned brown.

Lisa checked the seals and the pressure gauge to see if there was air on the other side. It checked out and she cycled through. A musty, fishy smell caused her empty stomach to swell with nausea.

She swallowed the urge to vomit and set to work on broken equipment. She needed to quickly increase the power drain. Plus, Royce's mention of a food scarcity had raised the resource higher on her list of priorities.

Lights came on in patches as she repaired them. Able to see, she fixed aerators in the fish tanks and gathered dead fish into a bucket to take to the reclamation unit. As she went from one to the next, she swapped out the algae filters.

A vat of fingerling sized, algae-eating fish didn't have a food source, so she put the used filters there for them to clean. Moving on to the air circulation units, she discovered that none of the fans were moving. Lisa opened the nearest motor casing to find that dust contaminated the compartment. She brushed it clean with a rag from the floor, then traced everything out. The bearings had seized.

She moved to the next unit. It looked fine, but the fan wouldn't turn. Rust had corroded every surface in the room.

She pulled a spray can of lubricant from her toolkit and sparingly applied it to the junctures. Then she grabbed two of the fan blades and tugged, breaking loose the rusted connection. Now the blades turned freely.

She worked more grease into the moving parts before engaging the motor. It started, squealed, and smoked for a moment, but then ran smoothly. The increased circulation would keep the plants' respiration of carbon dioxide going and the people breathing oxygenated air.

She looked around, planning her next task. Just then, Royce strode into the hydroponics bay with a fussing baby on his shoulder. Lines of concern creased the corners of his brown eyes.

"He's sucking his fists." He patted the infant's back.

"I'll nurse him." Lisa climbed from her knees and dusted them off. "But maybe I'd better wash my hands first." She hurried to the nearest sink and scrubbed with a brush and soap to remove the grease from beneath her fingernails.

Cegory's cries increased in volume. Lisa's breasts tingled. Was her milk letting down?

"He's not patient." Royce stepped in to unbutton her shirt with his free hand.

"What are you doing?" Shocked, she pulled her hands from the water.

"He won't stop screaming." Royce thrust the baby toward her exposed breast.

She accepted the child into her arms and guided her nipple into his mouth. Cegory latched on with dizzying speed. Royce stared at a wet spot that had formed on her uniform top where her other breast had leaked through the fabric.

Embarrassed, Lisa turned away. Royce reached around her body and pulled the shirt away from her breast. Maneuvering for a clear view, he cocked his head.

"The fluid is white now." He thumbed her nipple and tasted the liquid. "It's sweet."

She froze in humiliation. "Why would you—" Her words choked off as impotent rage brought on tears.

"I–I was curious." He covered her breast with the shirt.

"Please, allow me some dignity." She swallowed her sobs.

"What does that word even mean?" His frown deepened. "Slavery strips all of that away. You're lucky to have clothes. Colonial slaves are never covered."

She wept openly in mortification. He gaped at her response. Finally, he guided her out of the hydroponics bay.

"Come over here and sit down." He brought her to a dirty but comfortable recliner. "I've made breakfast. Are you hungry?"

"Yes, and thirsty." She adjusted the baby in her arms, relaxing for the first time in hours.

"It's seaweed soup." Royce brought her a glass of water and a bowl of nourishment.

"May I have a drink first, please?" Her mouth watered in anticipation of the soup, but she couldn't feed herself with only one free hand.

"Sure." He handed her the glass and then started spooning the soup into his mouth. "It's good." He slurped more of it. "It has a savory, smooth flavor." He finished it off.

Hungry, she watched his every move.

He seemed to notice. "There's more."

"Thank you." Relieved, she settled in with the baby. "I'll come over and have some after the Cegory is fed. I love seaweed soup. We eat it in SEVEN often since it's so nutritious." She glanced at him. "But I'm sure you know that already."

"I made it for you as a way of apologizing." He set his spoon in the bowl.

"I appreciate the gesture." She changed the subject. "What are your plans for the baby?"

"Are we going to survive, then?" He adjusted his stance.

"Air pressure has stabilized." She raised the darling infant to her shoulder and patted his back. "Oxygen levels are improving since one of the circulation fans is working again. I still have a lot to do, but I'm optimistic."

"I'll take care of Cegory while you work." Royce squared his shoulders.

"Does he eat solid food?" She lowered the baby to her other breast.

"Yes." Royce ladled soup into a clean bowl. "I gave him soup, but he wasn't satisfied."

"I increased the lighting." Her stomach grumbled in anticipation. "Of course, that doesn't help anything today. But soon, things will grow and produce."

"Not as fast as you have." He held up his free hand splayed in cupping shape. "You're enlarging by the hour."

"Please, don't talk about my body that way." She looked at the baby, nursing at a breast that had easily doubled in size. "It makes me uncomfortable." Holding Cegory soothed her even in the midst of her devastating circumstances.

"What makes me uncomfortable is liars." Royce set the bowl on the counter.

"Well, that's lucky because I don't lie." She scowled at him.

"Oh, yes, you do." He met her scowl with one of his own. "You aren't really Korean."

"Genetically, I'm fourteen percent." Most people in SEVEN had Asian ancestry and maintained those ancestral traditions to varying degrees. "But culturally, I'm as close as a Martian can come."

"That doesn't mean you should deceive people into thinking you're Asian." His eyes narrowed and his lips pressed together in a harsh line.

"I dye my hair black because I'm trying to represent who I am inside. It isn't meant to trick anyone." She blinked rapidly.

"You're a blonde Caucasian." He clenched his jaw. "This is why clothes weren't allowed in the slave quarters. It's honest. We hide nothing."

"Modesty isn't the same as deception." Lisa ducked her chin in shame. "I color my hair because I was ridiculed for being Caucasian. My father looks Korean and so do many of my siblings. I just wanted to be like them."

"I know the real reason." Royce faced her. "You resent your Caucasian mother's heritage. It's never made sense to me. At least, you have a heritage. You have a family that loves you." He walked away. "It's foolish to reject the person who loves you the most."

Lisa watched him go as his words sunk into her heart. She'd always justified it, but she was wrong to have rejected her true ethnicity. Wracked with remorse, she wished with everything in her that she could apologize to her mother right now.

Chapter Eighteen

Royce cycled through to the passageway that led to the locker room and jogged toward it until he reached the first airlock on the right. Keying in the code, he entered the pressure chamber and looked out into the scrapyard. The faint light of morning entered through the large doors across the vast space.

Everything he owned was out there, well, other than his children, Lisa, and the things he'd taken from NINE. Flaco owned the facilities chamber and hydroponics bay. He'd robbed air pressure from the yard's chamber to maintain them. There wasn't much of a choice since the equipment there kept everyone alive.

"Is it much further?" A boy's voice carried along the corridor behind him.

"The lady doesn't that weigh much. Quit complaining." Flaco's boots stomped along with the softer footfalls of Royce's son.

"Mother?" Royce stepped into the corridor.

"What did you say?" Flaco and the boy pulled up short.

"Is that my mother, Addison Albright, from the medical rover?" Royce stared at the black body bag.

"I guess so, since the other body was a man." Flaco made room for Royce to take the body. "We'll bring him next."

Royce took Addison's body in his arms. She didn't weigh much because she wasn't much taller than Lisa. Powerful women came in small packages.

"Thank you." He made eye contact with his son. "Drift, she was your grandmother. Will you come to the reclamation ceremony?"

The adolescent boy nodded. Flaco sighed, nodding his approval. Royce had rescued too many of his children to be able to care for them all, so he'd fostered them out to trusted friends.

"Radio me when it's safe to return." Flaco motioned for the boy to go with Royce.

"It's safe now." Royce headed back with his mother's body. "Lisa sealed the breach and has fixed half the broken equipment already. You owe me a fortune."

"I hope you don't mind if I go back to work then." Flaco tromped the other direction.

Royce carried his mother's body into the facilities chamber. Lisa had dozed off in the reclining chair with the baby in her arms. At least, she'd managed to eat her bowl of soup.

He strode past on his way to the reclamation chamber with Drift following close behind. Mounting the steps, he laid his mother on the platform and unzipped the body bag. She looked well enough to let the boy see her.

"Come on up, Son." He adjusted his position to allow the boy to come up between the hand railing.

Drift obeyed, looking at Addison. "I know her. She was on the vid. She's the head of the Gold Council."

"True, but she was also the head of the resistance, my mother, and your grandmother." Royce set a hand on his son's shoulder. "I served her, and she gave her life for me. The Matchmaker is her father. He abused her the way he did me. She was a brave woman."

"What killed her?" Drift faced his father. "The other guy was blasted through the head, but there isn't a mark on her."

"A kill switch is meshed with her brain." He turned her head so the boy could see the small incision behind Addison's ear. "The Matchmaker murdered his daughter."

"We have to stop him." Drift tensed. "Why won't you let me go to the front lines?"

"If I didn't love you, then I'd let you go." Royce hugged the boy. "But it's my job to protect you. I don't have much time left to be your father, so let me at least keep you safe for a little while longer."

"I can take care of myself." Drift descended the steps. "I'm not a child."

The baby fussed, and Drift took Cegory from Lisa's arms. Startling awake, Lisa sat up straight in the chair. Her gaze darted around the chamber.

"Come pay your respects to your mother-in-law, Lisa." Royce used the firm tone Alik had employed when he expected to be obeyed.

Agape, she glanced at Drift, turning pink cheeked at the boy's bold gaze. She arose and stalked across the chamber, doing as commanded. Elbowing up next to him on the ladder, she struggled for breath.

"I'm not your wife." She whispered.

"But you were my brother's." Royce hadn't intended to tell her this way, but it felt right.

Her jaw fell open. Wide eyed, she searched his expression while her chest heaved for air. Slowly, her gaze shifted from him to his mother.

"You asked me what I knew about her." Lisa stared at Addison's face. "She married Fortney Greene right out of high school. They had four children, three girls and a boy." Lisa glanced at him. "Five children, counting you." She looked at Addison again. "She kept her maiden name, causing Cody a great deal of resentment. That's why I eventually took Cody's name. You keep calling me Shim, but I'm a Greene now." She straightened her spine. "Addison Albright's position within the government explains why Cody kept her identity a secret."

"Her position within the resistance is why she concealed Cody's existence." Royce stared at his mother, wishing she could answer more of his questions.

"Why was I never told about the resistance?" Lisa looked at him.

"Your parents didn't want their children placed at risk." He inhaled a deep breath. "I might as well tell you that your mother is the lead judge in the absentia court. She's the one who issued me orders of execution."

"What?" Lisa's knees buckled.

Royce pulled her against his body, holding her upright. "She didn't order me to kill you. That was all my idea. I apologize for my mistake."

Unsteady, she hyperventilated against his chest. He adjusted position, sitting on a step with her on his lap. Holding her like this made him wish for things he knew would make her heart race.

"Why didn't my mother tell me?" Lisa's voice came out breathy.

"You can't keep secrets." He kissed her forehead.

"Did Cody know about the resistance?" She pulled her arms against her chest.

"Not likely." Royce refrained from caressing her face. "It's a small movement within the colonies."

"And the outlaws?" She looked up at him.

"There are outlaws who keep to themselves out here." He discretely wetted his lips with the tip of his tongue. "And there are militant revolutionaries seeking to overthrow the government through any means necessary. The night I took you from NINE, they attacked the elites on the Glass Highway. Radio chatter indicated that they killed nearly half of them before they could enter the Incursion Zone."

Lisa grasped Royce's shirt with both hands. "What Incursion Zone?"

"Gail Crater." Royce smoothed her hair back from her face.

"No." All the air left her chest, and she fell limp in his arms.

He realized how powerful his love for her had become. She had always been a dream, an ideal, the woman he hoped to meet. Now, she was right here in his arms and he couldn't have her because if he did, he'd destroy her.

"Is she the Lisa you always talked about?" Drift drank hot soup from a cup. "I thought she'd gone bad."

"Yes, Son. She's the one." Royce carried Lisa down the steps and gently laid her in the reclining chair. "But I'm the one who went bad for a while. She never did anything wrong. I only thought she had."

"So, you're in love with her?" Drift bounced the baby on his shoulder.

"Yes, she's the only woman for me." Royce stared at Lisa's chest to be sure she was still breathing.

"But you can't have her." Drift strode to the table. "That's rough."

"I could still do plenty with her." Royce faced his son.

"Enough to make a marriage legal?" Drift met his gaze for a moment out of the corner of his eyes.

"Yes, with a shield, I think it would be legal." Royce stood up straight. "If she'd consent."

"Ah, that's the difficulty, right?" Drift scoffed. "Women."

"What do you know about it?" Royce caressed Lisa's cheek.

"I know that Shade strung Alik along right until the end." Drift shook his head. "Then, after you called in Cody's location, suddenly she said yes to marriage. They said their vows right before they loaded in a rover together and led the crew. Before they were out of sight, she was on his lap in the pilot seat, giving him what he'd always wanted. But she didn't love him."

"Yes, she did, Son." Royce clenched his jaw. "She was simply afraid of intimacy."

"Everything they left you will be divided by the crew when you die." The boy clenched his fists. "Father, if Lisa's half the woman you think she is, then marry her and leave your holdings to her. I don't care what bargain you have to strike, we all need her."

Royce knew he meant all of the children needed a mother. He'd brought Lisa here for that purpose. Unfortunately, she was never going to surrender her heart to him let alone her body.

"The law is clear about consent." Royce mounted the steps of the reclamation chamber.

"Then romance her." Drift carried Cegory over to the chamber, both of them looking up at Royce.

"How?" Royce removed his mother's clothes and shifted her body into the internment cylinder. "I'm a push button romantic."

Drift chuckled. "Well, that's not what a good woman wants. She needs to know that you care about her more than you do for yourself. She's going to ask you to rescue Cody. When she does, make the deal for her body alone. Let her keep her heart."

"But she has mine." He bowed his head in prayer, hoping that God would understand the necessity of what he must do.

"And that's eternal, I guess." Drift adjusted his stance, avoiding Royce's gaze. "Unfortunately, it won't be long before you're laying up there, and I'm dropping you in. Don't leave us defenseless."

"I'll keep you safe, Son." Royce recited the burial prayer from the Bible and pulled the leaver that dropped Addison's body inside the reclamation chamber.

Chapter Nineteen

Light entered Cody's bedroom through drapes at the end of the room. The peach color of the window coverings warmed the space like an old earth sunrise. He wasn't sure when that had happened, but it had dispelled a nightmare.

For that he was desperately grateful because in his dream, Andrea had been taking a sample from him by natural means. It was one of those dreams where you can't move or speak even though you're trying to escape with all your might. He'd never had a nightmare become erotic before, and the sensations disturbed him, especially when he realized that his bottoms were wet.

He climbed out of bed and walked to the bathroom. Stripping, he used the toilet and the shower, washing away the creepy feeling that lingered even after the dream.

Dressing for the day, he felt better. Maybe today the team would find a cure for the Rot. He strode over to pull the curtains.

A white wall of mist swirled on the other side of the glass. He stared into the light, fascinated by an occasional pocket of clear air that gave him a glimpse of the landscape below. Plants grew around red sandstone boulders. The crater's vastness astounded his senses.

He'd descended thirty levels to arrive at his mother's residence. The Gold Council was stealing air and water from the colonies, jeopardizing everyone's lives, because they wanted to live in the open air. The selfishness of it twisted in his gut, especially since the instant he'd seen those plants, he'd had his hand on the glass yearning to be out there among them.

In the growing light and thinning mist, a figure waded through the greenery. She wore a yellow, low pressure suit and gathered purple fruits into a basket. Through her clear helmet, he saw that she had her hair tied back the way Lisa liked to do.

For an instant, his heart leapt in his chest, thinking it was her. But as the woman drew closer, her Asian features were more pronounced than Lisa's. He recognized Sahra, Lisa's next younger sister.

He banged on the glass to draw her attention. Her head turned in his direction and cocked to the side as she waved awkwardly. Looking up at him from below, she hesitantly moved in his direction.

He pressed his palms to the glass before deciding to go down to let her inside. He hurried through the apartment to a spiral staircase. Descending to a large, ground-floor livingroom with an airlock, he placed his hand on the security scanner to authorize Sahra's petition to enter the residence.

She cycled through, maintaining eye contact as she carried her basket of fruit into the room. "Did Lisa survive the coma?" Her helmet distorted her smooth, alto voice.

"Yes." He took the basket of fruit from her hands so she could unseal her helmet. "Lisa awoke five days ago like nothing had happened. In fact, she refused to believe me at first."

"Sounds like her." Sahra laughed delightfully. "Is she here?" She looked around the room, holding her helmet under one arm.

"No, not yet." He met her gaze, holding it in seriousness. "An outlaw took her into the Northern Territories. But, don't worry, I'll find a way to go after her soon." He set the basket on a knee high table by the floral print sofa.

"Are you certain that's best?" Sahra set her helmet beside the basket. "I mean, are you sure she isn't better off out there?"

"I don't know." He had considered that possibility. "There's a complication. The outlaw has the rot and infected the Matchmaker. Reports from NINE say that he may have infected Lisa as well. We're searching for a cure right now."

"Then–" Sahra straightened her posture. "You work for your grandfather?"

"No." Cody shook his head, emphasizing the point. "I do not work for criminals. I'm not part of the Gold Circle. I only want to help Lisa. Since she may be infected, I must do everything I can to find a cure. Many people are dying from this disease. It's important work." He swallowed his resentment at her accusation that he'd changed loyalties, but it stung, especially since she must be the one who had betrayed Lisa by stealing a copy of the resource transfer protocol before it had been destroyed.

"At least, you have something interesting to do." Sahra sat on the edge of a sofa cushion. "Now that the plants are in fruit, my crew picks and processes all day long."

"Well, that's good honest work." He grabbed a piece of the purple fruit and took a juicy bite.

"No." Sahra sprang forward, grabbing the fruit from his hand. "Spit it out."

He obeyed despite the delicious taste, catching the unchewed piece in his free hand. "What's the matter?"

"Spit out all the juice." She pulled his shoulder forward. "It has to be processed before it can be eaten or it causes a serious fever."

Embarrassed to spit in front of her, he went to a nearby half bath's sink to do it. Throwing the piece in his hand in the trash, he washed his face and hands with soap. Sahra stood in the doorway with a fresh piece of fruit.

"You have to wash it with soap, peel it, and then spit out the seeds." She washed it, pulled the purple skin off of it, and offered him the clear, juicy inside.

He ate it, collecting the seeds in his mouth before spitting them into the trash can. "It's delicious."

"My father created the strain." Sahra smiled as she washed her hands. "It grows in low atmosphere with very little light and moisture required, propagating in three ways like a strawberry plant." She dried her hands. "Of course, like most things, if you water it, provide ample sunshine, and fertilize it, then it grows faster." She seemed to notice his proximity and backed out the doorway, returning to the sofa.

"Is it the only thing growing out there?" He followed her and sat in an overstuffed chair.

"As soon as the atmospheric pressure will sustain it, we'll be planting normal varieties of trees and plants." She glanced at her sandy boots. "I'm sorry. I'm afraid I've tracked dirt all over the cream colored carpet." She stood, heading for the airlock. "I should go back to work."

"Don't worry about the mud." He followed her. "When can I see you again?"

"Maybe tomorrow morning." She sealed her helmet.

"Don't forget your fruit." He rushed to grab it from the table.

She took it and cycled through the airlock, waving goodbye. He waved in return. Her warmth, openness, and intelligence reminded him of Lisa, but without as much of the social awkwardness. He wished she'd stay.

Chapter Twenty

Lisa often went to sleep pondering a problem and awoke with a solution. Despite the fitfulness of the baby beside her on the makeshift bed, she had rested. That's when the answer came to her in a dream.

"Royce." She arose and walked over to him at the table he used for cooking. "Light therapy boosts the immune system, and I think it will slow the spread of your sores."

"Lisa, I'd like you to meet my son, Drift." He stepped aside to reveal the adolescent boy mincing mushrooms and chives on the other side of the table.

"Oh, it's nice to meet you." Lisa bowed slightly.

"I'm glad to meet you too." He smiled and kept working. "My father talks about you all the time. He thinks you're pretty special."

"I'm an engineer, that's all." Lisa liked the boy right away. "It's just a job. There's nothing uncommon about the profession."

"Sure, there isn't anything exceptional about you at all." Royce grinned. "Lisa, you're too modest. Drift is fully aware you invented everything that makes this planet amazing."

"Oh." She ducked her head.

"I grew up in the colonies." Drift shrugged. "Everyone knows who you are."

"Well, I'm a slave now, so none of that matters anymore." Lisa couldn't keep the resentment from her tone.

"You don't have to be a slave." Drift glanced at Royce. "Marry my father and you'll be free. Plus, everything he owns will be yours in a few days." The boy held her gaze expectantly.

"I'm in love with Cody Greene." Lisa held her ground. "I'm committed to him. I might be carrying his child. I respect your father, but I can't marry him."

"Widows can remarry." Drift's eyes filled with tears. "Please, you have to do this."

"Son." Royce rounded the table to take the boy in an embrace. "I won't die without making sure you're well cared for. You like Flaco. He's a good guardian, right?"

Drift broke from the embrace and stalked over to flop on the rag bed next to the baby. Cegory awakened with a shrill scream. Drift shook his head, but picked up the infant, taking him for a walk in the hydroponics bay.

"I'm sorry about that. He's just worried." Royce whipped powdered eggs with water, added chopped ingredients, and poured the mixture into a skillet. "I'm making Korean pancakes for breakfast."

"How many children are you responsible for?" Lisa came up to the table, wanting to be useful and enjoying the smell of the food.

"Seven, counting Cegory." Royce readied a spatula to flip the omelette-like Korean dish. "I pay mentors to care for them, but upon my death, they'll be divided along with the rest of my holdings since I don't have a wife."

"Will their mentors keep them?" It made no sense to her.

"Most of them can't afford to." He flipped the pancake.

"Then what happens?" She grabbed a plate.

"Drift is my oldest. He'll join the revolutionaries. The rest are pretty helpless. They'll starve." Royce scooped the pancake onto her plate. "Some of the scrapyard crew are mentoring two at a time. You're the only one within my holdings old enough to inherit upon my death."

"How did you inherit Alik and Shade's holdings?" Lisa cut the pancake with chopsticks and inhaled the aroma from the hot bite that still needed to cool before she dared to eat it.

"I served as Alik's steward." He chopped more chives and mushrooms.

"I could do that for you." She offered him the bite on her chopsticks.

"Not really." He accepted the bite she offered, chewing with a smile on his lips.

"Why not?" She cut another bite and ate it.

"You're not a man." He whipped up another pancake.

"No, I'm a woman. Why does that matter?" Lisa knew she was missing something, but as usual couldn't quite span the gap when it came to social constructs.

"The laws in the Northern Territory are quite sexist." Royce poured the mixture into the sizzling skillet. "It's mostly men out here. Women are rare commodities. If you want to inherit my holdings, then you have to marry me of your own free will and choice." He cleared his throat. "And couple with me at least once."

Lisa's throat closed up, causing her to choke. "I won't do it."

"Then someone on the crew will claim you." He poised the spatula to flip the pancake. "But I doubt they'll offer to marry you. Slaves don't have the right to refuse sex to their husbands. They'll just exploit you until you're all used up and then drop you in the reclamation unit."

"That's your law?" Outrage swelled in Lisa's chest until she couldn't contain it any longer. "Rape is legal here?" She came around the table to jab him in the chest with a finger. "You could rape me, and I have no recourse? That's not right. You know that's not acceptable. You're a better man than that."

"I agree." He chuckled nervously, avoiding her pointy finger as he flipped the pancake. "I'm just letting you know how important it is that you marry me, Lisa." He took her hands in his. "I'll wear a shield. I won't hurt you."

She shuddered with dread at the very thought of him penetrating her body even if it was only once. Cody wouldn't understand her choosing to be unfaithful. It would destroy him.

"I can't." She struggled to catch her breath, fighting for air with lungs that refused to obey her wishes.

"They'll use you, buy you, sell you, and if you fight them, they'll punish you." He held her close. "I can drug you, if that helps you to relax enough to accept me."

"The pancake is scorching." She stared at it in the pan.

He scooped it onto a plate, holding her up with one arm. He shut off the heat. With a sigh, he pulled her close and rubbed her back until her breathing calmed.

"I'm not dead yet." He released her from his embrace. "You have some time to think about it."

Drift flung open the door to the hydroponics bay, holding the screaming Cegory. His gaze locked on Lisa, and he marched the baby over to hand him to her. Both he and the infant were drenched.

"What happened?" Royce tensed.

"This crazy baby decided to dive out of my arms into a fish tank." Drift wrung out his shirt. "I had to go in after him."

"He'll be fine." Lisa shushed the baby, concealing a smile. "Infants start doing that sort of thing at this age. They have no fear."

"Well, I do." Drift came up beside her, looking at Cegory. "He scared me to death."

"You're very brave for rescuing him." She smoothed Drift's wet hair back from his forehead. "I can't swim and water scares me."

"It wasn't deep." He met her gaze. "It was like a cold bath or something only fishy."

"I fixed the clothes washer and dryer." She offered him a smile. "Maybe you should go take a shower."

"You're not going to look, are you?" He stood there dripping.

"Of course, not." She stripped Cegory of his wet clothes. "Please put these in the washer with yours."

He took the clothes and did as she asked. She turned her back, snuggling Cegory to her breast. The showerhead on the wall by the sink came on and Drift started to sing.

"He's a good boy." Royce cooked a third pancake.

"I'm impressed with him." Lisa shifted her attention, looking the baby over to be sure he hadn't been injured. "I don't think Cegory is Asian."

"Why's that?" Royce came over.

"Well, if he were my cousin's son, then he would probably have a blue bottom." Heat flushed her cheeks to talk about a baby's backside with a man, but that's how she'd formulated her opinion. "Besides, he looks just like you."

"Or Cody." Royce met her gaze. "We are brothers after all and look alike." He eyed the baby. "What's this about a blue bottom?"

"It's a genetic trait with some Asian's, like a birthmark, only it fades as the child ages." Lisa cuddled the baby to keep him warm. "He needs a bath. Will you heat some water on the burner? I haven't had time to fix the water heater yet."

"Sure." Royce strode over, grabbed a pot, and filled it with water. "He hate's cold showers."

"Is that what you usually do?" She burped the baby and put him on her other breast.

"That's what Shade did." He set the pot on the burner. "He probably hasn't had a shower since she died." He frowned. "I should have done better with him."

"The clothes won't be ready for a while, but breakfast smells good." Drift strode over wearing nothing but a towel. "Can I have some?"

"Eat it while it's hot." Royce handed him the freshest pancake.

"Wow." The boy ate it by hand. "This is good. Is there more?"

"Not today." Royce shook his head with a slightly amused expression upturning the corners of his lips. "But if Lisa like's my cooking, then I think I'll keep her."

The bottom dropped out of Lisa's stomach. Royce looked so much like Cody. He even sounded like him.

And here he was cooking like him. Suddenly emotional, Lisa fled with the infant to check on the washing machine. Though, clearly, the brothers resembled each other, they were not the same man. Yet, Royce even smelled like Cody.

She splashed cold water on her face. Cegory fussed at the rude treatment. How on Mars could she even be considering Royce's proposition?

Chapter Twenty-One

"Lisa, are you all right?" Royce came up behind her at the sink.

"Yes, Master." Lisa shushed the baby. "I'm fine."

"Please, call me Royce." He turned her around by the shoulders to face him.

"You have to at least try to live." Lisa dried her face on her sleeve.

"How?" He held out his hands at his sides in question. "What were you saying about light therapy?"

"The human body has an amazing capacity to overcome disease." Lisa strode toward a dark colored lightbulb embedded in the far wall.

"So, you think a sunlamp will help?" He eyed the large bulb.

"I think wearing a shock suit and then an environmental suit, both of which block the light, caused your condition to deteriorate rapidly." She rummaged for eye protection.

"You could be right." He nodded. "I only had a couple of sores before I started wearing suits."

"The bulb is intense when you stand close to it, so we'll need these." She put protective goggles over her eyeglasses, handing him a second pair.

"All right." He put on the goggles. "How long do I need to stand here?"

"Um, well, only five minutes at a time." She avoided his goggled gaze. "And it would be best if you exposed the sores to direct light, I think." Her cheeks flushed.

"Nothing but goggles on." He chuckled. "Is that how you like it, Neesa?" He captured her gaze amused by her suggestion.

"No." She tilted her head. "The goggles are protective gear."

"If you want me to use protection..." He swaggered over to stand directly in front of the lamps. "I'm more than happy to oblige."

"Please, do." She poised her finger over the light switch. "But I think it would be best if Drift takes Cegory into another room for a few minutes."

"So we can be alone?" He winked at her.

"Yes." She frowned.

"You're just the way I imagined." He unbuttoned his uniform top, provocatively flexing his chest.

"What does that mean?" She wrapped the baby in a blanket and handed him to Drift, who left the room.

"It means that you focus on only one thing, and I'd like you to focus on me." He unbuttoned his bottoms, lowered the zipper, and teasingly lowered his undershorts.

"Make sure the effected area is bathed in light." Lisa pressed the button and the light came on.

"Would you like to do that part?" He finished undressing and flashed her a smile.

"No." Her brows crashed together as she glanced from his goggles to his groin and back again. "Are you asking me to handle you? That's highly inappropriate, don't you think?" She took a step backward.

"No, it isn't." He met her gaze from behind the dark goggles. "I need your assistance, and since you like to help people, I thought you might make this easy for me."

"I'm sure you can manage it just fine." She took another step backward.

"That's a lot less enjoyable than having you do it for me." He lifted this and shifted that, exposing the sores to the light.

"I don't understand why you keep saying things like this." She eyed the timer for the lamps.

"I was a sex slave from birth." He captured her gaze. "Unhealthy physical relationships were a part of everyday life. I want a healthy one with you. And, you need one with me. So, why should we deny ourselves a happy marriage no matter how short lived?"

"No, Royce." She curled inward, facing the light switch. "That is not the way things are supposed to be. Sexual relationships are sacred and should only be shared between a man and a woman who are legally married. It should always be consensual. Your experiences have taught you differently, but that is not the way of happiness. You will not find joy while doing wrong."

"I'm officially declaring that I'm yours, Lisa." He strode over and flipped off the light switch.

"I will never consent." She faced him, looking up his bare chest to meet his gaze.

"But part of you wants to, right?" He relaxed into an easy smile.

"No." She shook her head sharply. "That's not right."

"Oh, really?" He removed his goggles, and then he took off hers. "I know you better than that, Neesa."

Her breathing came rapid and shallow. Her gaze fixated on his lips. Leaning in, he fulfilled her unspoken request with a chaste kiss suitable for a sister-in-law. She held her breath.

"Breathe, Neesa." He gave her enough space to do so without withdrawing by much.

"You smell like Cody." She spoke softly.

"No two people smell exactly alike, not even identical twins." He kissed her again.

She kept breathing this time. In fact, her breaths came heavy and urgent as she returned his chaste kiss with one of greater passion. Reaching up to draw him closer, she tasted his lips with the tip of her tongue as if sampling him for comparison.

Pain shot through his groin as he responded to her in a way that he had never achieved without the stimulation device being activated. He tried to control it, thinking of filthy fish tanks and dirty diapers. He hoped it was working, but he didn't dare look down to check.

She ended the kiss with a final caress of her hand across his cheek. "You're more than his brother, aren't you?" She looked over his entire body, fixating on his midsection.

"You can't tell anyone." Royce covered his display with his hands. "Clones have no rights to anything but a swift death."

"The Matchmaker did this, didn't he?" Her brow creased with a delicate line in the middle.

"Yes." Royce ducked his head in shame. "My mother didn't know I existed until she found me in the slave lineup in a dungeon. Albert Addison is her father. Sometimes, he punished her by sending her there to be abused. Anyway, she recognized me right away and did her best to help me from then on. I didn't know I was a clone until the Matchmaker told me on the catwalk the other day."

"I-I can hardly believe it." She struggled to catch her breath. "I'm so sorry. Of course, I'll keep your secret for the children's sake."

"You will?" He stared at her with the deepest gratitude since the children would be executed too if the truth ever came out that they were half clones. "Thank you."

"And–" She picked up her goggles and his from where he'd dropped them. "I'll marry you before you die, according to the exactness of your law, but no more than that."

"What changed your mind?" A hardness entered his heart. "I don't want your pity."

"It's not pity." She put on her goggles. "It's obligation. Now put on your eye protection and do your best to live as long as possible." She poised a finger to flip on the lights.

"I don't understand." He put on the eye protection.

"Cody Greene, Royce Nedge, and Cegory Eden are anagrams." Lisa flipped on the light. "Who named you?"

"Shade suggested it." Why hadn't he ever figured this out?

"Then she was more intelligent than you gave her credit for." Lisa sighed. "What did they call you in the dungeon?"

"Bone." He cringed when she flinched at the word she'd feared since junior high school.

Chapter Twenty-Two

Cody left his mother's apartment to find Holden waiting for him outside the upper door. The scowl on his face spoke clearly of a foul mood, but he escorted Cody to the laboratory without voicing a complaint. Since it was later than Cody usually started work days, he decided to stay late to make up time.

Holden was never far away, but Cody ignored him. The research involved extensive reading in the overstuffed chair in the corner. When he found something interesting, he added it to the list of trial treatments.

By the end of the day, he'd found twenty natural substances to use on patients. Since everything else had already been exhausted, the doctors agreed to the strategy. Each trial started immediately upon approval, and all of them included a healthy dose of sunshine.

Cody and the other nurses wheeled patients around the mostly deserted promenade. The worst off were on gurneys, but the children were healthier and most of them were in wheelchairs. The fresh air and natural lighting beneath the transparent aluminum latticework did everyone good.

A fog had clouded his mind ever since his mother had jabbed him with the sedative days ago. Of course, it didn't help that someone had dosed him again after capturing him at the border. Even still, he should be feeling clear headed by now.

He sat on a bench beneath a palm tree. Reaching out to rub the rough trunk, he took comfort that at least his favorite trees were here with him. The fruity air current circulating through the breeze way smelled like a concentrated version of the purple fruit Sahra had given him.

He hadn't seen any Shim bushes on the promenade, but Sahra's crew must be processing the fruit somewhere. That would send the smell throughout the ventilation system. Inescapable.

Fortunately, the aroma was heavenly. He draped his arms across the back of the bench and turned his face to the setting sun. The young girl with him followed his lead, both of them soaking up as much as possible before night fell.

"All right, everyone." Director Tran strode up to the group in her white lab coat. "Time for baths, treatments, and bed. We'll all be back here first thing in the morning for more sunshine, though. So, no complaining." She eyed Cody.

"Yes, Director." He released the breaks on his patient's wheelchair and did exactly as she'd asked.

Everything took longer than expected due to the protective gear required when working with infectious patients. By the time he arrived at his mother's apartment, he was exhausted. After a quick shower and a brief prayer for Lisa's well being, he pulled back the covers to find that someone had changed the sheets.

It was the last pleasant thing he remembered thinking before he fell into bed. Almost immediately, the nightmare involving Andrea started again. Only this time, the woman who mounted his hips was a stranger.

Chapter Twenty-Three

Lisa finished fixing the essential equipment in the facilities chamber. She'd been forced to improvise a few of the solutions, but now even the backups were functional. Looking around at the tidy chamber, she absent mindedly rubbed a sore breast.

She'd awakened on the floor this morning engorged and in terrible pain. Only Cegory had improved the situation, but at a cost. Her nipples ached from the unaccustomed suckling.

Royce had offered to help. His impish grin had caused a flash of desire to plant in her core that irked her greatly. She'd politely declined his offer.

Drift had helped to clean the place up. He'd been careful to collect even the tiniest spring or nut so that the hope of fixing the secondary backups remained. It wouldn't due to sweep up useful parts and toss them into the reclamation unit.

"When will the scrapyard crew return?" Lisa sat in the chair to nurse the baby.

"I'll ask how many more wrecks they have to haul in from the battle." Royce strode over to the wall mounted radio unit, leaning in to send a coded message.

Drift knelt next to the medical kit, pulling out a tube of diaper cream. Suddenly, he reached deeper into the bag again. Staring at an object, his expression grew serious.

"Father, what is this?" He raised the locket from the kit.

Royce ended his call. "Alik gave it to me."

"Why?" Drift stood with the locket in his hand.

"He said I needed to reclaim the control that had been robbed from me." Royce took the locket and put it around his neck, tucking it inside his uniform top. "I used it in NINE to stay alive." He shrugged. "My customers never noticed."

"That's why you're sick?" Drift's expression darkened.

"You don't think I actually wanted any of them, do you?" He glanced at Lisa. "I just needed a false identity to access NINE, formula for Cegory, and an occasional meal to keep me going while I assassinated criminals."

"They paid you for sex, right?" Drift scowled. "And you caught the Rot."

"I should have asked my mother for help." Royce frowned. "Then I wouldn't have had to earn my way by compromising my principles."

"Now, she's dead." Drift clenched his fists. "And soon you will be too."

"I did what I thought I had to do to hunt down the Matchmaker." Royce sat on the edge of the table, folding his massive arms across his chest. "I was wrong about Lisa's involvement and for that I'm sorry. Unfortunately, remorse doesn't change the consequences, and I won't be around to raise you. That's my biggest regret. Luckily, Lisa has agreed to marry me as a means to make things right with you and the other children."

"She did?" Drift met Lisa's gaze.

"Yes." Lisa had agonized over the decision, but it was the merciful thing to do, no matter how undesirable the compromise. "You asked me to marry your father. Does that mean you will accept me as your guardian?"

"Sure, but I thought you would become my new mother." He cocked his head to the side, squinting at her.

"Of course, Drift, I will become your new mother if that's what you want." Emotion choked Lisa at the hope that he intended to accept her as a parent. "I only used the word guardian out of respect for your real mother."

"Well, I hate her, so don't bother." He clenched his jaw. "I want a new mother, not someone like her."

"Son, Lisa is nothing like your mother." Royce laid a hand on Drift's shoulder. "You'll be safe, provided for, and loved." He glanced at Lisa. "If you're really nice to her, she may even take you out of mentorship and keep you."

"Drift, you don't have to be nice to me to gain my love." Lisa buttoned up her shirt and stood with the baby in her arms. "You already have it. I think you're a wonderful boy and I want you to be with me. What I need from you is honesty. So, always tell me what you think, how you feel, and what you'd like to have happen. Can you do that?"

Drift nodded. He hugged his father, burying his face in Royce's chest. Then, he broke away, striding into the hydroponics bay.

Chapter Twenty-Four

"Trina, how did you contract the Rot?" Cody tucked the little girl into a bed in the pediatric hospital ward after another long day, sat in a chair, and prepared to read her a bedtime story.

"I think it happened while I was sleeping." The kindergarten aged girl frowned. "Mommy's friend gave me candy, and I woke up hurting." She looked Cody in the eyes as if asking for an explanation.

"I'm sorry your mother's friend hurt you." Indignation surged in Cody's chest. "Was he a man?"

"No." Her frown deepened. "Mommy said that what the woman did helped us because we needed credits for rent."

"Where is you mother now?" Cody would make sure she and the child molester faced justice for their crimes.

"The police man said Mommy drowned." The child stared at him from her position on her pillow. "She worked at the water treatment facility."

"I'm sorry, Sweetheart." He had been the rescue diver who pulled the body from the pump's intake. "Where's your father?"

"I don't have one." The little girl's eyes filled with tears.

"Well." Cody opened the book. "You have me, and I'll keep you safe from now on." He read the story about a boy and his pet turtle three times before Trina fell asleep.

Kissing her brow, he prayed over her. How could anyone harm this sweet angel? Her long, brunette hair and big, brown eyes had melted his heart from the moment he'd met her.

Praetorius had killed her mother. Executed her for her crimes, was more like it. Suddenly, things made more sense.

Cody set the book on the bedside table and left the lamp on, quietly exiting the large room full of sleeping children. An orderly mopped the floor in the hallway. There were nurses at the station nearby, and of course Holden waited to escort him back to his new home for the night.

"If she asks for me, don't hesitate to call." He spoke to the young nurse on duty. "I left a book by her bed. She seemed to like it."

"We'll take good care of her." Nurse Hasklin nodded with an understanding smile.

"Thank you." He reluctantly returned to his mother's apartment, dreading his dreams tonight.

Chapter Twenty-Five

Royce confronted Flaco the instant the man returned to the facilities chamber. "What took you so long? I need an environmental suit."

Flaco took a defensive stance like the seasoned Space Division fighter he had been before he joined the cause of freedom. "You still owe me for the hours of complaining your son forced me to listen to. If I had half as many grievances as that boy, I think I'd shoot myself."

"Try it." Royce scowled, taking the criticism of Drift personally. "I'm sure you'll enjoy the lump on your head almost as much as you appreciate the two day headache that comes with it."

"Now, don't take offense." Flaco held his hands up. "The boy just talks too much for my taste."

"Well, you won't have to worry about that for long." Royce relaxed his balled fists. "I'm marrying Lisa. She's planning to raise the children."

"How's that going to work out?" Flaco scratched his head, causing the flop of dark hair to shift back and forth.

"You're the law expert." Royce faced Flaco with his back to the chamber where Lisa and Drift stood around the table serving green salad to the crew that had arrived right before Flaco.

"I read up on the particulars to pass the time out in the barrens." Flaco shook his head gently with a serious look in his distant gaze. "If neither of you has been sterilized, and you consent to couple with the intent of producing a child, then the declaration of marriage is legally binding."

"Neither of us is sterile, but what does that second part mean exactly?" Royce's anxiety level raised along with the tension in his shoulders.

"I think it's pretty clear." Flaco eyed him in an odd way. "You have sex without using contraception."

"I can't use a shield?" Royce's heart pounded in his chest.

"Right." Flaco shuffled a foot. "What do you think the chances of her being infected are?"

"Why?" Royce grabbed the man by the shoulder.

"If she's infected, then Cegory will be too." Flaco shoved Royce away. "It could spread."

"You and the crew can't have her." Royce menaced the wiry man.

"None of us will want her in that condition." Flaco straightened his shirt. "Is there a chance she's pregnant?"

"Yes." Royce resisted the urge to pound the man into a pulp.

"Well, then, the second stipulation might already be fulfilled." Flaco glanced at Lisa and back to Royce. "Use the shield to couple with her. That way, if she turns out to be pregnant later on, it won't matter that you've gone into the reclamation unit."

"You'll honor the marriage?" Royce's mood lifted with hope.

"None of us will touch her." Flaco squared his shoulders. "Unless she bleeds or never shows around the middle. But by then you won't be around to care what happens." Flaco strode toward the salad.

Royce stalked toward Lisa and Drift to stand behind them with his arms folded across his chest. Lisa had tied the baby to her front with a blanket. The little one slept peacefully with his ear to her chest.

Royce would kill anyone who tried to hurt the one's he loved. He simply wouldn't be here when they tried. That left God alone to defend them...unless Lisa was pregnant with Cody's child.

Chapter Twenty-Six

Cody didn't dream of Andrea. Instead, he dreamed of his brother's wrath rained down on a woman who had sold her young daughter to a child molester. He dreamed of taking justice into his hands like Praetorius.

Whatever drove the man must be a tortured past. The pornographic recordings of children that Cody had found in THREE had a boy in many of them that looked like his brother. Why had their mother allowed that to happen?

No answer came to mind because something impossible to ignore happened to his body. Heat, suckling, and a rhythmic motion held him in its sway. Opening his eyes a slit, he hardened in the unfamiliar woman's mouth despite his efforts to fight his response.

She teased and molested his entire body until at last she straddled him, standing on the bed naked. Then, she lowered her body, taking him in and rocking like a jockey riding a horse. He wanted to stop her.

He'd do anything to prevent his physical reaction to the stimuli forced on him. But when she climaxed, he followed right behind her to his shame. He couldn't help it.

Neither could he make her go away. She lay on top of him, panting for breath. Taking his hand to her breast, she used him to caress her body.

"That's enough." Andrea jerked his hand from the woman's grip.

This wasn't a dream. The evil woman dismounted in a violent motion, causing pain. Holden grabbed hold of her upper arms.

"I wasn't finished." The woman flirtatiously caressed Holden's jawline with one hand, unzipping his pants with the other.

"Yes, you are." Holden shook her once and shoved her toward the door.

"I'm telling the Matchmaker what you've done." The woman raised a fist at him.

"You do that." Holden leveled his stun pistol and fired on her, turning to Andrea as he zipped up his bottoms. "Was that as good for you as it was for me?"

Andrea's worried expression didn't lighten. "She'll receive worse punishment than that from the Matchmaker if she's broken his penis."

Holden winced. "Can that happen?"

"Yes." Sitting on the side of his bed, Andrea inspected Cody's body with tenderness. "It feels normal, but I'll have to check again in a few hours for swelling or bruising." She sanitized all of his exposed skin with wipes and pulled up his bottoms.

"Andrea." Holden came down on a knee beside her, taking her face in his hands. "What are we doing?"

"We're saving his life." She knelt in his full embrace.

"So you can be with Lisa?" Holden held his wife close.

"No, not anymore." She rested her head against his shoulder with her lips caressing his neck. "You're all I want now." She looked at Cody. "Though, I know you feel differently."

"Well." Holden glanced at Cody too. "I thought he was what I wanted for so long that it became a habit. I can't tell you when it changed for me, but you are the reason I want a normal family."

"Normal?" She wrapped her arms around his middle.

"You, me, and a baby." He caressed her face, turning his head until their lips nearly met.

"Just us?" Her lips brushed his.

"Yes." He kissed her tenderly, parting slightly. "I love you, Andrea."

"One moment, please." Andrea separated from him enough to take him by the hands. "Holden Martin, are you saying you actually love me?"

"I told you this wouldn't happen, but I was wrong." He chuckled.

"Words of affection aren't often spoken in Asian cultures." She wiped tears from her cheeks. "But I want you to know how very special you are to me. I treasure your sense of humor and I love you." She met his gaze. "With my whole heart."

"I like the sound of that." Holden smiled puffing out his chest. "Now that we have that straight, help me drag this sex offender out of here before Cody wakes up."

The two of them hauled the degenerate woman away. Paralyzed, Cody lay there considering the misery of his existence. Without Lisa, he would never be happy again.

Unfortunately, he wasn't sure he could ever deserve her. How could he endure this kind of humiliation? He must fight back.

Chapter Twenty-Seven

Lisa harvested mature lettuce leaves from the hydroponics bay plants. Drift searched the dark corner mushroom patches for the tasty fungi. And a very sick looking Royce carried Cegory while teaching a passel of his young children about raising fish.

"Daddy, when is breakfast?" A little girl tugged on his hand.

"Well, Lydia." He hefted her up onto his shoulders. "We'll be having salad in just a few minutes."

"Rabbit food?" A little boy made a face.

"I'd rather eat a rabbit." A larger boy grabbed the air as if catching an animal.

"I have a pack of dietary chews in my back pocket." Royce held onto the daughter on his shoulders' feet.

"You do?" Several of the little children said as they searched his pockets.

Lisa finished her task, watching him kneel to put his daughter down with Cegory in her lap. He then cut the six round dietary chews in half so that each child received a serving of vital nutrients. It broke her heart because it wasn't sufficient, and the plants in the hydroponics bay were growing, but not fast enough to feed this many people.

"Thank you, Daddy." The children wrapped their arms around Royce, holding their pieces in their little hands.

"You're welcome, Dear Ones." With a look of utter exhaustion, he patted their backs and kissed their heads. "I'll find some more food today when I go out into the scrapyard."

"But there's no air out there." A little boy's face went pale.

"I'll wear a suit." Royce patted him on the head. "I'll be fine. Now, go wash your hands and prepare for breakfast."

With no complaints, the children enthusiastically headed toward Lisa at the sinks. Fortunately, she'd finished rinsing the lettuce leaves. Shaking the water out of the strainer she held, she carried it into the facilities chamber to the table and set to work making them a meal.

One by one the children ran into the room to line up behind the scrapyard crew. Drift followed soon after with washed mushrooms. Last of all, Royce came in, carrying the baby.

Lisa chopped chives, mushrooms, and lettuce leaves, tossing the mixture in an enormous bowl that had once been part of an engine's shielding. The scrapyard crew took heaping servings, leaving little for the children to share. Before Royce's turn to eat, everything was gone.

"Well, I see that you've managed to please everyone but me." He winked at her.

Tears pricked in her eyes. "I held something back." She showed him the small mushroom hidden in her hand.

"You thought of me?" He took her hand in his, looking down at the mushroom in her palm.

"I know you haven't eaten." She ducked her head, neither had she, but until a few days ago, she'd had plenty and was still in good health.

He took the mushroom, leaving an orange dietary chew in its place. She stared at the gift as he chewed the mushroom. Trembling and on the verge of tears, she prayed for God to bless him.

Chapter Twenty-Eight

"Flaco, sell me back my suit." Royce hurt everywhere, but he boldly crossed the crowded facilities chamber and reached into his pocket for tokens. "I'll go into the scrapyard and release more air from the tanks. Then we can cross over to the canyon."

"No deal." Flaco rubbed the stubble on his chin. "Besides, I doubt there's enough air in the wrecks we just brought in to bring up the pressure."

"Not the new ones, but the chamber has been full for years." Royce clenched his fists. "Most of the old junkers have air pressure in their systems. Rent me the suit if you won't sell me one."

"Only if you run it down to the locker room for sanitization afterward." Flaco took a wary stance.

"Agreed." Royce handed Flaco five tokens. "If I do this, then I'm charging you double at the shade tree."

"Succeed." Flaco smiled a lopsided grin. "Or I'm charging triple for that mushroom you just ate."

"That's ruthless." Royce's mood lifted.

"Aye, it's piracy." Flaco laughed and handed him the suit from among his pile of belongings.

"You owe me a fortune for having Lisa fix this place up." Royce tallied it up in his head.

"Not true." Flaco's merriment ended. "All she did was make up for the mess Shade made."

"That's a filthy lie." Royce menaced the smaller man.

"Fine. I take it back." Flaco grumbled as he walked away.

Royce strode the opposite direction in search of Lisa to tell her his plan. Little ones ran all over the place, most of them harassing Drift into going out to play a seek and find game in the hydroponics bay. He felt sorry for the boy, except that he seemed to enjoy their admiration.

Crossing the chamber, Royce spotted Lisa sitting on a blanket in a somewhat secluded spot under the platform of the reclamation chamber. Cegory lay at her breast, and on either side of her napped two other tiny children. He unfolded a large scrap of tattered plastic and secured it to the open side of the platform, creating a semblance of privacy.

"Neesa, what's wrong?" He spoke softly in Korean, coming inside the shelter to kneel at her feet.

"I'm fine." She wiped a continuous stream of tears with a white cloth. "It's just hormones."

"Oh." He pulled a sealed groin shield from his front pocket. "I only have one."

"That's the last thing I want right now." Lisa sobbed.

"I'm confused." He drew closer. "To me hormones means a need for physical release."

"That's certainly not what I meant." She avoided his gaze.

"I was about to put on an environmental suit." He didn't want her to worry while he was gone. "I have to go out into the scrapyard to release air from the wrecks to bring up the pressure. I'm planning on taking you and the children across to Alik's residence. So, don't cry about our situation. You'll like it there. It has hot water."

"May I help you?" Lisa's tears slowed. "I need to scan for air leaks." She lifted the baby on her shoulder to burp him. "You wouldn't want to waste your reserves."

"The scrapyard holds air pressure." He crawled over the top of her legs to deliver a kiss on her cheek. "I only rented one suit. Besides, it looks like you're busy." He glanced at her breasts.

"These babies need mother's milk, too." She laid Cegory on the blanket nearest to the warmth of the reclamation unit.

"Neesa, you can't nurse all three." Royce parted her uniform top to inspect her breasts. "Especially without a steady diet of healthy food."

"I must." Lisa raised her knees, pulling them against her chest. "Timmy is barely walking, and Mia isn't much older. Their brains won't develop properly without milk."

"I didn't know that." Royce sat in front of her, taking her hands.

"I'm being careful." She met his gaze. "I'm only nursing them in the morning, at nap time, and before bed."

"Your health won't last." He put his legs around her and pulled her forward until she knelt in front of him.

"I'll be fine." Her breath came quicker.

"Neesa." He traced her eyebrow with his fingertips, pushing her long dark hair behind her ear. "Please, become my wife today."

"Are you asking to consummate our marriage in a crowded room?" Lisa spoke Korean, turning a deep shade of pink.

"No one can see in here." At least, he hoped they couldn't, but it didn't matter because he knew death was coming for him soon. "I think this is my last day with any strength."

"Royce, you have to live." She grabbed his shirt front with both hands, drawing close to him.

"I would if I could." He slid his hands up the back of her shirt to caress her skin.

"Today's not a good day." She made no move to stop him.

"I think its for the best." He kissed her lips, tasting the salt of her tears as he massaged her back.

"Then I consent." She kissed him slow and deep.

He gently palm her breasts as she unbuttoned her top. Granted access, he slowly kissed down her neck. She raised up to place a nipple against his lips.

Her skin smelled of milk and babies. Tenderly, he caressed each breast with his lips, experiencing a reverence unlike anything he'd ever felt before. He loved this woman.

"I wish I wasn't sick." He adjusted her position until she sat straddling his lap.

"I do too." She leaned against his chest, hugging him around the middle.

"Right." He tensed at her words. "Because then you wouldn't need to marry me today."

"But we must marry." She unbuttoned his uniform top all the way down to his bottoms and kept going.

"Careful." He held her hands away from the infected skin.

"All right." She moved back a bit, holding her top closed.

"You only need to settle onto me once." He lowered his bottoms down his thighs.

"Will this hurt you?" She stared at the swollen sores.

"Only for a moment." He draped the full groin shield across his lap, sliding his shaft into the tight sleeve of protection.

"What are the chances of a breach?" She met his gaze.

"Very little, we won't be coupled for long." He wished it could be otherwise, but this was their agreement.

"Oh." She stared at his lap while she removed her bottoms, then ducked her head. "I'm sorry about the mess." She braced her feet on either side of him and raised up a little.

He grabbed her bare hips before she could commit to him, spotting a trace of blood issuing from between her lovely folds. Desire battled with the need to confess that their union wouldn't be legal since she wasn't pregnant. Instead, he settled her against his body without penetration.

"This will be enough." He held her in his arms in an embrace he wished would never end.

"But I thought–"

He interrupted her objection with a lingering kiss that didn't last nearly long enough. Then, he shifted her modestly onto the blanket. Casting the shield aside, he pulled up his bottoms.

"I'll be gone all day, but check at the airlock once in a while for anything I might find to feed the children." He fled with the environmental suit and her toolkit to a safe place to mourn for the marriage he could never consumate.

Chapter Twenty-Nine

Royce jogged along the tunnel to the first airlock going into the scrapyard. Kneeling in prayer, he begged God to forgive him for taking advantage of Lisa. Why hadn't he told her about the need for a pregnancy?

She would never have let him do the things he'd done if she knew it was for nothing. The intimacies they'd shared were sacred. He understood that now.

He'd never made love to anyone before. Yes, he'd been abused by countless men and women. He'd even compromised his principles and sold his body, but he'd never been loved.

Lisa's trusting kisses lingered on his lips. She was willing to become his wife to save his children from starvation. She was sacrificing her health to breast-feed three of his babies simply so they wouldn't suffer.

He didn't deserve such a woman. He wasn't worthy. Yet, he needed her love, and her giving it had bonded him to her in a way he hadn't anticipated.

Married in the eyes of the law or not, he belonged to her alone. Or at least, he wanted to be hers. The only way forward was to risk infecting her or to be healed.

He prayed for a miracle and kept praying in his heart as he changed into the environmental suit. Grabbing her toolkit, he cycled through the airlock. Inside the enormous lava tube, he switched on his helmet's exterior lights and went wreck by wreck releasing air into the cavern.

Sometimes there was nothing more than the undercarriage storage compartment that still had air pressure. Once in a while, however, he found an intact life support system. Hours of effort had him sweating harder than his favorite workout, but he kept praying.

Every one of his muscles ached, but nothing hurt more than his groin. His condition had worsened throughout the day and hunger made it more painful. He needed medication, but so far, he hadn't found any.

He wouldn't forget which vehicles he'd already searched. But, the crew might decide to help him with this sometime soon. So, he'd marked each wreck with a grease pen from the toolkit.

Air pressure wasn't quite high enough yet, but he needed a rest. Sitting on the dirt floor, he leaned against the cracked and poorly patched observation bubble of a rover. Inside it, he spotted a lacy, white neglige along with other objects that littered the bloody interior.

This was the rover that had hit Alik and crushed Shade. Lisa must have been wearing that provocative undergarment when she changed into an environmental suit. He went around to pull wide the unsealed hatch, finding Cody's clothes on the deck too.

Those would fit. The thought took Royce by surprise. He pretended it wasn't hurtful to be another man's clone or to love that man's former wife.

Regardless, he needed something to wear and so did Lisa. Imagining her in the lingerie gave him a thrill. He fantasized about caressing the straps off of her shoulders until the skimpy thing landed on the floor.

Until today, she probably would have had something discouraging to say about such a fantasy. But he gathered the clothing and everything else abandoned in the wreck. Why hadn't the crew gleaned all this good stuff?

Maybe it was respect for the dead, but more likely it was grief. They seldom admitted it, but Shade had meant a lot to them. And like him, they'd practically worshiped Alik.

The driver's dead body had gone into the reclamation unit, but other than that, nothing had been touched. In fact, the life support system had full pressure. Lucky find.

Every compartment held air, too. He set about releasing all of it. When he reached the undercarriage, he hesitated.

Lisa's possessions would be down there, and releasing the air pressure might damage something important. If he was right, then he'd better wait to open it. He set his sack full of loot as well as Lisa's toolkit beside the wreck.

Light shone through the huge, transparent aluminum hatch of the secondary pressure chamber coming into the cavern. This side of the scrapyard wasn't used much anymore because it was full. Flaco must have put this rover here because he didn't want the reminder.

Alik had been everyone's idol, the model soldier, man, and leader. Shade had been everyone's surrogate mother. She may have messed up machines, but she knew how to mend men's souls.

Funny that she never resorted to physical contact to do it. No one other than Royce was ever allowed to touch her, and he'd only done so when the baby was born. All of Lisa's mother's births had been at home with family talking her through it in Korean.

Since no one on the crew knew anything about babies, Royce had become the designated doctor. Miraculously, it had gone well for both mother and child. From the moment he'd held Cegory in his hands, he'd loved him with a fierceness that stunned everyone. That's why Shade left him her son.

Royce walked toward the light. Once at the mechanic's bay sized hatch, he spotted greenery at the far end of the enormous interim chamber large enough for a wrecker and whatever it towed. Checking to be sure, he discovered that the chamber had equalized with the interior of the cavern instead of remaining a vacuum.

That meant there was a leak. Fortunately, it was on the interior hatch, not the exterior one. He could live with that until Lisa could fix it because at least they weren't losing pressure to the outside.

Keying in the code, he opened the hatch to find the cold outer door had condensation dripping down to the sand covered deck. Everywhere the moisture touched and enough dirt had collected, a plant had sprung up. Purple fruit grew on every bush.

Royce squeezed a piece, finding it soft as if ripe. It fell off the plant into his gauntleted hand. Without further encouragement, he gathered sacks and picked everything that seemed ready.

Closing the leaky door, he struggled as he hauled the fruit back to the tunnel airlock on the other side of the cavern. This would save everyone. He cycled through, removed his helmet, and ate three juicy pieces of fruit.

He'd never tasted anything like it. With a full belly, he left the rest in the alcove, and trudged to the locker room to sanitize the suit. Returning with the stowed suit in the nude, since he hadn't brought a change of clothes, he hadn't traveled far before he collapsed on the floor of the tunnel.

Chapter Thirty

Lisa left Cegory with Drift and went after Royce. He'd been gone too long. Flaco didn't care, but something about the situation had raised her concern.

Out of an abundance of caution, she took the medical kit. The airlock alcove had sacks and sacks of Shim fruit. Where had Royce found it?

Chewing her bottom lip, she wondered if he knew about the consequences of eating it without proper processing. Her father had warned his children about it. He'd nearly died after consuming a single piece of fruit.

His shame had been profound. But after he'd survived the fever, he had worked tirelessly to find a way to redeem himself. Washing, peeling, and removing the seeds had been enough to avoid the unwanted bacterial infection.

This much fruit would save everyone's lives. But where had Royce gone? The suit needed sanitized, of course.

She headed for the locker room, hoping to meet him on his return. If he'd eaten the fruit, then he could be dead already. If not, then he'd probably just be annoyed that her stubby legs would cost him time walking back to the facilities chamber with his treasure of fruit.

Unfortunately, no such hoped for reunion would take place today. The mumbling of a fever ravaged man reached her ears long before she found Royce spasming on the deck. The fact that he wore no clothes had saved his life in the chilly tunnel.

She grabbed a cloth and a small bottle of alcohol from the medical kit. Rubbing his body from head to foot, she managed to lower his temperature enough to ease the seizures.

"Lisa, what's wrong with me?" He met her gaze with the glassy eyed stare of the seriously ill.

"You'll be fine." She took his large hand in her small one, discomforted for an instant that it felt just like Cody's. "I'll take care of you."

"I'm in love with you." Trembling, he tugged her closer, but without any strength behind the effort.

"Don't give up. You can beat this." Lisa squeezed his hand without allowing him to draw her into an embrace.

"No." His head shook back and forth. "It hurts too much."

"I'll find something to help you." She rummaged in the medical kit with her free hand.

"Come to me, Neesa." He caressed the hand he held with his thumb. "Let me hold you."

"I'm trying to save your life." She discovered a packet of wet wipes in the medical kit.

"Why?" He squeezed his eyes shut and great tears raced down the sides of his head. "I'm a dead man anyway."

"I don't give up easily." She swabbed his brow, face, neck, shoulders, arms, torso, and skipped the central feature to continue with his legs and feet. "What else can I do?"

"Pray." His body spasmed, and he lost control of his hands.

"Dear Father in Heaven, please bless this man with comfort." She folded her arms and bowed her head, speaking in Korean. "If it be thy will, please, let him live to continue his fight for justice. Otherwise, help me to know how to ease his suffering. In the name of Jesus Christ, I pray. Amen."

"Amen." Royce passed out.

Chapter Thirty-One

Cody went about his days and nights in a drug befuddled state of dysphoria. The only thing that drove him forward or gave him any joy was Trina's little girl chatter. Unfortunately, her condition deteriorated and she eventually stopped talking.

A lethargy overcame her and she slept most of the time in the pediatric ward. He tried to entice her to eat, but she weakened. An intravenous line and a feeding tube kept her alive and medicated.

Despite every effort, her pains continued to increase. Cody stayed by her side through it all, reading countless stories and holding her hand. There was nothing more he could do.

In the end, Andrea came with a syringe of purple liquid to add to the line. "It might be too late." She pushed the fluid. "My only hope is that she's resilient."

"What is it?" He held onto the little girl's hand, finding a weak pulse in her wrist.

"Lisa radioed with a possible cure." Andrea's eyes pooled with tears.

"Shim fruit?" He leaned forward, looking at Trina. "I thought it caused a fever."

"Yes." Andrea pulled up a chair on the other side of the bed. "It's serious. Her little heart may give out. Most of the adult patients have died, but through trial and error, we've reduced the risk for Trina and the other children."

"God gave Lisa the cure." He stroked the birthmark on the little girl's hand. "Does that mean that Praetorius will survive Rotcargathogen too?"

"Lisa's message didn't say." Andrea brushed the hair back from Trina's sweaty brow.

"I think it's implied." He clenched his jaw. "Now, let's make sure Praetorius' daughter survives as well."

Chapter Thirty-Two

Royce awoke wrapped in a blanket on the floor inside Lisa's shelter in the facilities chamber. She sat beside him, nursing Mia. She met his gaze with a slight smile that didn't reach her eyes.

"I'm alive." He had no idea how.

"And so are we, thanks to you." She pulled the plastic drape aside for a moment to show him the children running around the chamber energetically. "Where did you find Shim fruit?"

"It's growing inside an airlock in the scrapyard." He raised an eyebrow. "I found your white, lace lingerie too."

"Oh." She diverted her gaze as a blush colored her cheeks. "Well, that was for my honeymoon night with Cody. I don't usually–" She looked him in the eyes. "Hey, did you find my ancestor's table?"

"Maybe." He folded his arms behind his head, catching her attention by baring his chest from beneath the blanket. "I figured your parents would have given it to you, so I left the compartment sealed. Wood splits with radical changes. I didn't want to damage it."

"Thank you." Warm emotion filled her voice. "I thought I'd lost it forever."

"What's mine is yours." He grinned in triumph. "As long as you let me have a look at you in that neglige."

"I will not." Lisa startled the toddler with her adamant response, causing her to cry.

"Let me have her." Royce sat up.

"She hasn't had the other side yet." She handed his daughter to him, covering her chest and buttoning her top.

"There, there, Mia." Royce soothed her with a rocking motion. "Everything is right in the world." Surprisingly, the words rang truer than he'd thought. "Why do I feel so good? Did you drug me?"

"Yes." She smiled briefly with a twinkle of mischief in her eyes. "But the fever reducers wore off hours ago."

"Then, I'm going to live?" He cocked his head.

"It looks that way." She took his hand.

"What?" He snuggled Mia against his chest, taking comfort in Lisa's touch.

"The sores are gone." Lisa smiled openly.

"Really?" He glanced downward, pulling the blanket away for a look. "What's that?"

"Iodine." She hurried out into the facilities chamber to the sink, returning with a wet washcloth. "It isn't permanent."

"Oh." He cradled the baby. "Prove it."

"I'd rather feed Mia." She reached for the child, trying to hand over the washcloth.

"She's content where she is." Royce spread his knees, crossing his ankles with the toddler held high above his lap.

"Royce, please." Lisa met his gaze.

"You've obviously been handling me plenty already." He accepted the washcloth and relinquished the child. "Why stop now?" He washed his groin until most of the iodine was gone. "Looks like the sores are dried up."

"Fevers are the body's way of fighting infection." She settled Mia at her other breast.

"What caused the fever." Royce rubbed at the remainder of the iodine.

"Shim fruit." Lisa watched him rub.

"I ate three pieces." He scrubbed at a stubborn stain in a crease.

"It has to be processed before it can be eaten." She stared. "The fever has been known to cause death."

"Is it known to cure Rotcargathogen?" Royce marveled at his lack of pain. "I haven't felt this good in weeks."

"The moment I noticed your sores begin to heal, I radioed the possibility to the colonies." She finally blinked. "Andrea radioed back this morning that the treatment she refined had cured everyone who survived the fever."

"Cured?" He couldn't believe it.

"Yes." She continued to stare at his manly attributes.

"Then, I'm yours, Neesa." He rested his hands on his knees.

"What?" She met his gaze.

"If you still want me." His heart did something strange in his chest.

"We don't have to marry." She avoided his gaze.

"I guess that means you don't love me anymore." His heart thudded in his chest.

"I never said I loved you." She released Mia to toddle out into the room.

"You made love to me." He had trouble speaking past the lump of emotion in his throat.

"I satisfied the law." She stared at her hands in her lap without buttoning her top.

"No, you didn't." He gathered his courage. "The law didn't require that level of intimacy."

"No, it required more." Color flooded her cheeks.

"You're not wrong." He ran a hand through his hair. "We're required to couple with the intent of creating a child. The use of the shield was only permissible if you were pregnant."

"Oh." She hugged her knees to her chest. "That explains why you didn't go through with it."

"I didn't want to take advantage of you." His heart quivered in his chest.

"But that's what you're asking now, right?" She stared at her feet.

"I love you." His hands trembled with the need to touch her.

"Why?" She faced her head the other way.

"Because you're so special." He raised his knees and crossed his ankles, blocking her view of his groin.

"I betrayed Cody's trust." Enormous tears formed in her eyes, splashing her cheeks the first time she blinked.

"I am Cody." He whispered.

"You're nothing like him." Anger flashed in her eyes, though she spoke softly.

"I'm exactly like him." He came forward to kneel in front of her, pressing the green button inside his cursed locket. "You see him when you look at me."

"No, I don't." She raised up on her knees, meeting his gaze without flinching.

"Then what about this do you like so much?" He held her gaze.

"I–" Her chest heaved with several breaths. "I think you're–" She shook her head, looking away.

"I'm what?" His heart pounded in his chest.

"Perfect." She unclenched her fists and rested back on her heals. "I think you're the most perfect man I've ever seen."

He scoffed. "A spatial anomaly worthy of experimentation."

"Yes." Her gaze locked with his. "Add to that the emotional elements involved, and I would have chosen you over Cody if not for your trying to kill me. But I choose him before I knew you. I made love to him completely. That's why I'm not going to be intimidated, enticed, or convinced that becoming your wife will be anything other than a betrayal of my vows now that–" She clenched her jaw shut.

"Ah, there it is." He sat back, covered his groin with the blanket and pressed the black button, groaning in pain. "You needed an excuse to love me, and now you don't have one." He laid down in a mild state of paralysis.

Her nostrils flared, and her small hands formed fists. Shaking her head, she stared straight at the plastic sheet. Without warning, she climbed to her feet and marched out into the room without a backward glance.

Chapter Thirty-Three

Cody awoke to the sound of children playing in the pediatric ward. Laying against the side of Trina's empty bed, he lifted his head. Laughter bubbled from the little girl's lips as she ran around playing a game with the other pediatric patients.

"Trina, you're alive." He stood, instantly light headed from lack of quality sleep.

"I'm all better." She giggled and chased her friends.

He chuckled, adjusting his gaze to take in the rest of the room. Andrea stood in the doorway. Meeting his gaze, she folded her arms across her chest.

Light came in the wall of windows, revealing swirling clouds rolling off a distant waterfall dropping from the southern lip of Gail Crater. The Glass Highway joined the bridge at that juncture. Water was still being taken from the colonies, though not as much as when he first arrived.

"It's time for a nap." Andrea pulled the vertical blinds across the window and closed them.

The children grumbled, but laid down in their beds. Cody tucked Trina in, laying a kiss on her brow. Fatigue lined her young face and she closed her eyes, cracking them to look at him only once before sleep overtook her.

"We need to go." Holden held a pulse rifle at the ready.

"Where?" Cody hoped it was someplace other than his mother's apartment.

"To a private hospital room." Andrea led the way along an unfamiliar section of the hospital.

"Why?" The hair on the Cody's arms stood on end.

"Ask the Matchmaker." Andrea swiped a door key, granting them access to a secure room.

"Where is he?" Cody's blood pounded in his ears as he charged inside.

"I'm watching via camera." The Matchmaker's voice echoed in the sterilized room. "You look tired, Grandson." The old man chuckled. "Have a rest on the bed."

Four orderlies rushed at Cody, but he wasn't going down without a fight. Holden and Andrea stood back, though Holden leveled his weapon at the orderlies as if he might fire but never did. The brawl left broken equipment as well as men, however, the result was Cody strapped naked to the bed.

"Doctor Tran, have you increased my grandson's sperm count." The Matchmaker's voice came from a speaker mounted in the wall.

"Yes, a little." Andrea avoided meeting the men in the room's gaze. "However, my research indicates that waiting longer between matches would yield better results."

The able bodied orderlies carried their injured companions out the doorway. Holden stood guard. Andrea gestured for him to go outside.

"Fine." He glanced from her to Cody and then shut the door.

"Why haven't you been using the stimulator?" The Matchmaker asked.

"A more gentle approach is required in his case." Andrea's neck flushed with color. "He's had ample sunlight, exercise, and sleep." She choked on the last word.

"Yet, you haven't complied with my orders for the last two nights." The Matchmaker's voice held disapproval.

"I'm sorry, sir." She ducked her head.

Cody struggled against the restraints until his wrists and ankles chafed bloody. Rocking the bed, he tried to break it free of the anchors that held it fast to the floor. Suddenly the restraints moved until his arms and legs were spread in four directions and he was unable to move anything but his head.

"Demonstrate your gentle touch approach." The Matchmaker's voice grated darkly.

Andrea sorted through cabinets and drawers, pulling out a syringe and a vile of medication.

"No sedative this time." The Matchmaker tisked.

"Please, don't make me do this." Andrea cringed as if in pain, grasping her head with both hands.

"Do it." The Matchmaker laughed. "He's not a fool. Surely, he already knows what you've been doing to him."

"Don't kill me." Andrea's knees buckled. "I'll do it."

"Good. Now, strip." The Matchmaker's voice purred. "For my benefit."

"Yes, sir." She swept the hair back from behind her right ear to uncover the fresh incision of the neural mesh implant to Cody's view. "I'm sorry about this, Mr. Greene." Andrea slipped off her shoes and unzipped her bottoms, removing them along with her socks. "I've been facilitating matches while you sleep." She grabbed a tube of gel. "If I want to live, then I do what I'm told."

"Are you pregnant?" Cody's outrage lowered his tone to his deepest range.

"Not as of a blood test this morning." She squeezed gel into her palm and laid the tube on the side of the bed.

"Stop." He tried to avoid her reach. "Don't you dare."

"I'm not doing it for you." She grasped hold of him.

"Then why?" He resisted the warming effects of the stimulant and tried to pretend like she wasn't massaging him the way she was. "It's not for Lisa's sake anymore."

"I'm doing this for Holden." She pumped him until he responded. "They'll kill him if I don't comply."

"So you're going to force me to have sex with you?" He flexed every muscle he had in an effort to break free.

"Remove your top." The Matchmaker's voice filled with anticipation.

"Yes, sir." Her hands trembled as she complied.

Chapter Thirty-Four

Lisa strode out into the scrapyard with her toolkit ready to forget the unmanageable mess she'd made with Royce and focus on the doable problem of fixing rovers. The crew had taken turns tending him through his illness while she worked for the past two days. Well, they had started to help after it became clear that he was cured.

They'd also been eager to earn credits selling refurbished rovers to the resistance. Of course, she had focused on support vehicles rather than assault craft, but they needed everything and were glad to pay for it. She hadn't mentioned to Royce exactly how rich she'd made him, but he'd find out soon enough.

Eight rovers had gone out the airlock in the past thirty-six hours. News traveled fast and half a dozen pilots had been dropped off just this morning. She watched them hunt through the wrecks for a craft that suited their needs.

The first one who flagged her down received her full attention. That pilot and the hungriest scrapyard crew members helped her lay into a troop transport. Whatever it needed, they scavenged from rovers she'd designated as for parts only.

Within three hours, the pilot signed over ownership of a dozen crates of shelf stable food stuffs and drove away in his coveted transport. She paid the crew in tokens for their time or traded them food. Pushing past exhaustion, she lined up the next job.

Chapter Thirty-Five

Royce determined that if he wasn't going to die, and Lisa wouldn't marry him, then he would finish his mission to kill the Matchmaker. All of this misery had been caused by that man. It had to end.

Andrea Tran had the cure. The Matchmaker would send for her. That meant the window of opportunity to do something would close as soon as the Matchmaker recovered enough to flee to the Incursion Zone.

Fortunately, Royce knew something few others did. Andrea served the resistance as a double agent embedded in the Gold Circle. She had a weakness, though.

She loved her husband. Since the Matchmaker had the man, he likely controlled the woman. Thus, she'd probably give the Matchmaker the cure.

Royce hoped the fever killed the old goat, but he couldn't take that chance. He had to infiltrate NINE. Though, he wasn't sure Cody's credentials would still work.

Leaving Drift in charge of the little ones, he carried a fussing Cegory out of Alik's residence where he'd moved the family today. Heaving a sigh, he used the evening feeding for the baby as a pretense to see Lisa. He intended to glean information from her about NINE's security protocols and how to bypass them, but more than that, he missed spending time with her.

"That's another one down." Lisa smiled at Flaco as she wiped her greasy hands on a rag from her back pocket.

"I asked you to work on the assault vehicles." Royce strode up to her and the crew, carrying Cegory in his arms. "He's hungry."

"I'll feed him." She accepted the boy and faced away from the men to nurse the infant while standing. "I worked on nonlethal rovers first because they're useful in the event of a colony failure."

"Then you've given up on rescuing Cody?" Royce's right hand clenched.

"No, I certainly have not." Lisa met his gaze.

"I've studied the maps." Royce held firm. "I know Gail Crater. But there are too many laser outposts guarding it. We need the will of the people. Imagine how many craft we would have if everyone understood what the Matchmaker has done."

"Many of them know and don't care." Lisa's shoulders sagged.

"They'll care about their lives." Royce straightened his spine. "They'll stand up to the threat if they realize where the danger is coming from."

"The Matchmaker is still in NINE, and no one has done a thing." Lisa held Cegory close.

"The colonists don't know who he is or the seriousness of the crimes he's committed." Royce clenched a fist. "I'm going back to execute him for his crimes."

"Radio the information." Lisa touched his arm. "Don't go."

"Space Division controls the receivers in the colonies." He looked around at the crew. "Our contacts have gone silent, right? We haven't heard anything in days."

"Right." Flaco nodded with his head down.

"Then, we need to infiltrate NINE and force a public confession from the Matchmaker." Royce scanned the faces of the crew. "The severity of his crimes will sway the colonists to join the resistance."

"He'll finally pay for what he's done." Flaco cracked the knuckles of his left hand.

"I would go back with you if I could." Lisa rubbed the scar behind her right ear. "But they'd kill me in an instant. So, I'll keep repairing rovers. Drift can help me."

"You want to go with me?" Royce contemplated the terrifying idea.

"Yes, you'll probably need me." She sighed. "But since that's not possible, I'll tell you a secret way into NINE. I found it while scanning for heat leaks. On the north wall of the central tube, there's a false rock. Lift it and descend eight floors to a storage room. The computer will challenge your identity, and you'll have to authenticate before going any further."

"How does that help the crew break in?" Royce's jaw muscles bunched.

"Well, I can clone your identification by linking all of you together with transmitters." Lisa glanced at the five men looking at her. "That way, you will all become undetectable to the authorities."

"We can't just drive up in a rover because NINE is on high alert." Flaco said.

"Can you make it close enough to walk?" Lisa buttoned her top.

"Maybe, but it would take half a dozen assault vehicles as support." Flaco frowned. "The revolutionaries might provide the pilots if we can repair the extra vehicles."

"That's easily done." Lisa burped the baby, facing the crew. "So, if you can ride in close enough, then you can walk in at night covered by a radar shield. Once you make it to the fake rock and descend to the storage room, Royce will authenticate. Your devices will clone it for all of you. From there, you can execute a plan to capture the Matchmaker. He'll probably be hiding in the second floor hospital." Lisa wiped her brow. "Of course, all of that depends on there being air in sub-level eight."

"And if there's not?" Flaco looked at her curiously.

"Then Royce won't be able to pass the palm scan." Lisa handed Cegory to Royce. "Shall we set to work on those assault vehicles?"

Royce nodded along with the other men. They would work through the night to prepare for the mission. Lisa wasted no time, striding off into the scrapyard.

Royce watched her go, then carried Cegory back to Alik's residence. Did she care that he was leaving? Looking at his little ones running around much past their bedtime, he dreaded bidding them farewell in the morning.

Chapter Thirty-Six

Cody lay strapped to the hospital bed for two days. After Andrea finished exploiting him and left the room, the Matchmaker sent a parade of women to his hospital bed. Each one did as his grandfather instructed with fear in their eyes even though he sometimes could be heard snoring on the other end of the communication connection.

A nurse stayed to supervise his safety and clean his body between women. She wasn't permitted to leave the room. He'd wondered why.

"Now, little Nurse Hasklin, mate with my grandson before I release you from your duties." The Matchmaker's voice held triumphal amusement.

The nurse's blank expression took on a look of utter dismay as she stood without complying. Two orderlies entered the room. Fighting hard, she soon succumbed to the brute strength of the men subduing her resistance.

The two men ripped her clothes off without regard for injury. Weeping and trying to cover her body with her arms, they tossed her into bed with Cody. Shaking from head to toe, she cowered beside him.

"Why are you doing this?" Cody locked gazes with the lead orderly. "She's barely out of high school." He shifted his address to the receiver. "Grandfather, leave her alone."

"And if I do?" He paused. "What will you do for me?"

"What more do you want?" Cody dreaded the answer.

"Marry a Shim."

"Have you recovered Lisa from the Northern Territories?" His heart raced with renewed hope laced with intense fear.

"Lisa is lost to us for now." He sighed. "But Sahra Shim is almost a perfect match and will be an excellent mother to your children. You could be happy together."

"What does she have to say about this?" He ground his teeth aware of the young nurse trembling in fear beside him.

"I'm sure she'll agree when faced with the possible deaths of so many loved ones." He chuckled.

"If I marry Sahra, then it's just her from now on." He glared at the receiver. "No, other matches. No, foursome. No, Andrea Tran or anyone else. And you leave us alone to raise our children in peace."

"It's a deal, as long as your first male child is trained to rule my empire." He laughed. "I'm about to receive the cure for the rot, and I look forward to grooming my successor."

"Only if you agree to never abuse any of my children." Cody had wondered where Andrea had gone, but she must be the one delivering the cure to the Matchmaker.

"I'll agree to that very difficult term." A throaty grumble sounded over the speakers. "But only if you will give semen samples whenever I require them to produce as many children as possible."

"What about me makes me so special?" He had to know.

"You are a genetic paragon cultivated for a hundred years." A giddy laugh spewed from the speakers. "Lisa and her siblings are an unexpected kind of genius. Together your genes will create a child worthy of ruling an empire and capable of expanding it in total control."

"So, the Martian Colonies have been a genetic experiment from the beginning?" He glanced at the wide eyed nurse next to him. "Let her go, and I'll agree to the altered terms."

"Done." A raspy cough followed the Matchmaker's word. "You drive a hard bargain."

The two orderlies, snatched Nurse Hasklin up by the arms and tossed her naked into the hallway. Holden went to her side, helping her up. The door swung closed with the two orderlies taking up positions on either side of it on the inside.

"Are you ready for your treatment, sir?" Andrea Tran's voice carried across the connection.

"Give that dose to Mambwe." The Matchmaker coughed deeper. "I want to be sure your cure works before I trust you."

"He's a more advanced case. The fever is likely to kill him." She spoke softly.

"I'd like to see that." He chuckled. "The fool's wife spread this thing to half of the orphanage in NINE. He deserves to die."

Cody strained against the restraints, incensed to learn that his friend and commander was married to a child molester. He'd worked for the man for years, rooting out corruption when the one giving him orders was in bed with the worst pedofile imaginable. It made sense now why they never found much hard evidence.

"I brought enough doses for everyone infected. With your permission, I'll administer them now." Andrea spoke in a subdued tone.

"Yes, make your rounds, but let me choose a dose at random first." Fatigue strained his voice.

"Of course, sir." Andrea sounded closer to the receiver.

"Good. I'll hold onto that. Now, go to work." The Matchmaker's breathing rate steadied and snoring noises commenced.

One of the orderlies switched off the communications device. "Time to shower you off and dress you for your marriage."

Cody's heart thudded in his chest. He hadn't bought enough time. The old man wasn't dead yet.

Chapter Thirty-Seven

Lisa knelt across from Royce at the short, Korean table of her ancestors. He'd retrieved it from the wrecked rover. Alik's residence was a spacious chamber sealed on the quiet end of the scrapyard and all of the children enjoyed their comfortable, new accommodations.

Drift knelt at her right, placing a pot of seaweed soup in the middle. Several children sidled up to the table as well. The baby lay on a blanket playing with his feet.

And since this moment was a great blessing, Lisa absorbed it with gratitude. She clasped her hands in her lap. Royce watched her with a quizzical tilt of the head.

She closed her eyes and bowed her head, saying a silent prayer. When she opened her eyes again, she ladled soup into his bowl, each of the children's bowls, and finally her own. Taking up her spoon, she noticed Royce's confused expression.

"What's wrong?" She laid her spoon on the table.

"Aren't you going to pray?" He frowned a little.

"I would be happy to." Lisa bowed her head offering a prayer of thanks where she beseeched God for good health and the strength to do his will.

"Amen."

Everyone ate in silence.

"The crew and finished the assault vehicles." Lisa ate the soup along with a bowl of rice and various side dishes, enjoying the feeling of a full stomach.

"You do excellent work." Royce ladled a second helping into his bowl.

"Thank you. Are you leaving this morning?" She suddenly had no stomach for food.

"Yes." He stared at his bowl. "I have something for you to take a look at while I'm gone."

"Oh?" She couldn't capture his gaze.

"Shade may not have been the best mechanic." He set down his spoon. "But, she had an untested hypophysis about how to restart the core. It was a moon brained idea." Royce's voice held tenderness. "Or so everyone thought, but she'd studied Earth as a girl to impress Cody." His eyes creased in the corners with a sad look. "Anyway, the moon fascinated her and she studied its effects on Earth's capacity to sustain life. Will you take a look at her research while I'm gone?"

Lisa nodded, unable to speak as her eyes filled with tears. He might not come back from this mission. Yet, it was the only hope of saving everyone on the planet from oppression.

"Thank you." He stood. "Will you take a walk with me? Shade's workshop isn't far."

"Of course, I will." Her fatigue didn't matter at a time like this.

Chapter Thirty-Eight

Royce lead Lisa out the rear airlock of Alik's residence into what everyone called the canyon. Inside the winding sandstone crevasse, Lisa stared at the stars above. He too marveled at the clarity of the view through the glass seal.

The uneven contours of the walls on either side spoke of ancient weathering. Wind and water had once flowed here, and it felt as if time still swam through the gap. This was his favorite place.

Climbing vines with bean pods reached for the starlight. The rustling of their leaves whispered forgotten secrets. How long had people lived in these passages?

The equipment Lisa had repaired in the facility's chamber circulated the air and supplied water for the plant life. However, the magic of the place still held him in awe.

"You confuse me." Lisa walked along side him.

"How so?" He spoke softly in this sacred place.

"You're so tender with Cegory and the other children." She avoided his gaze, demurely ducking her chin. "I know you love them. So, why leave? Why risk your life for vengeance again after God gave it back to you with such mercy?"

The deep sand leveled the floor of the canyon for them to walk. He trudged through the unaccustomed texture, enjoying it even though it slowed his progress. In the silver light, he marveled at the shadows and shapes of the natural rock.

"I have my reasons." Many of his children still needed rescued.

"There's something restful about this place." She caressed the irregular wall with her free hand. "Why not stay?"

"I would stay for you." He avoided her gaze, trying to protect his tender feelings.

"What are you asking?" She touched his arm.

"Marry me even though you don't have to." He faced her.

"Royce, I can't do that." She took his hand.

"Then, keep me here for another reason." He stroked her knuckles, nervous to make his request.

"What?" She looked up at him with her eyes reflecting starlight.

"Give me children." He didn't want to abandon the ones he already had, but the possibility of forming a solid family with Lisa tempted him.

"By artificial insemination?" She squeezed his hand.

"No, it has to be a genuine connection." He'd seen the product of cold unions with his other children. "You have to accept me physically. I know you can't love me, but I love you. It will be enough to form a bond inside which our children can grow up happy and secure."

"I will not be unfaithful to Cody." She shook her head, striding a few paces away.

"You saved my life." His heart pounded in his chest. "Explain to me why you did that and don't say it was for him."

"I care about you, Royce." She turned her back to him.

"If that were true, then you'd ask me to stay." He stared at her silhouette in the starlight.

"Thinking of you dying makes it so I can't breathe." She faced him, pointing at the center of her chest.

"Then don't let me go." He strode toward her.

"I have no right to ask you to stay." She shook her head.

"Do you love me?" He drew close without touching her.

"Yes." She held his gaze.

"I'm yours, Lisa." He smoothed her hair from her forehead. "I have been from the moment I first heard your voice."

"I can't be your wife." Lisa spoke softly.

"But you love me." The cruelty of it struck him in the center of his chest.

"You should find someone else." Her eyes glistened with tears in the gray light of early dawn.

"I won't." He embraced her, rubbing her back.

"I'm sorry." She wrapped her arms around his middle and held him tight.

"I am him, Neesa." He grasped her shoulders and met her gaze. "What does it matter which of us gives you children? I would have accepted his as my own if you were pregnant. There is no difference between Cody and I. We are the same man."

"Is that what you think?" She held his face in her hands. "Your creation didn't split Cody's spirit any more than Cegory's did. You are each a unique child of God. And I don't love you because you look like Cody."

"Then, why do you love me?" His greatest fear and insecurity laid bare.

"I love you because you are the man of my dreams." She caressed his neck and held onto his shoulders. "But, beyond that, you're a very special man, Royce. You deserve so much more than I can give. Someday, you'll find a woman willing to love you with her whole heart. It just isn't me."

"Marry me, Neesa." He gritted his teeth. "I will release you from your commitment the moment Cody is freed."

"No, Royce, I could never do that to you or the children." She reached up to draw him down until their foreheads touched. "I can't be your wife."

"Then kiss me once before I go." Tears splashed his face as he closed his eyes.

"Make sure you come back." She kissed his cheek, lingering with her breath on his skin.

Broken hearted, he left her for the last time.

Chapter Thirty-Nine

Showered, shaved, and dressed in dress whites, Cody stood, waiting to enter the wedding hall. Of course, after two days of torture, he couldn't stand without assistance. Two guards held him up on either side.

When the chime sounded, they hauled him through the doorway to meet his bride. Sahra stood there under guard, waiting for him in front of a Justice of the Peace with a camera crew broadcasting the event.

It felt like bigamy. Lisa was still alive. He still loved her.

This was wrong. It didn't matter that the law had stripped away legal standing of their union. He could never love Sahra, and she would probably never love him.

When the Justice spoke the words that bound them as husband and wife under the law, they both said yes. When told to kiss, they did briefly on the cheek. The Matchmaker cackled when Nurse Hasklin brought in a tray with two small cups of water and two pill packets, one holding a pink pill and the other, a blue pill.

"I'm looking forward to watching you take her apart in full color." Delirious laughter blurted from the speakers in the large, nearly empty room.

Sahra made eye contact with Cody as she swallowed the pill with the water. Nurse Hasklin had to help Cody open the packaging and hold his cup of water. He made a good show of swallowing.

"Check his mouth to be sure." The matchmaker's tone grew dark.

The guards pried Cody's jaw open. He fought the rough treatment to no avail. They probed with unwashed hands in every conceivable crevice of his mouth.

"Nothing." One guard reported. "He must have swallowed it."

"Fine." The Matchmaker could be heard drumming his fingers on an unseen surface. "Carry on."

"Yes, sir." The guard snapped his fingers and helped haul Cody off of his knees.

Sahra led the way to the elevator on their way to his mother's apartment, and Cody's guards dragged him behind her. Along the way, he locked his gaze on Sahra's hips and sprang at her. The guards escorting him laughed and held him fast as if they'd expected as much.

Once inside the elevator, Sahra whirled around and slammed against his body. Climbing him like a tree until her lips met his in a passionate kiss, she wrapped her legs around his body with an intensity that he matched with equal frenzy. Their bodies entwined so inextricably that the four guards couldn't separate the pair.

The camera crew angled for the best view in the tight space, exiting the elevator as soon as the door opened to pan out for a better shot. Writing with uncontrolled erotic energy, Cody and Sahra broke free of the guards' hold on them. She had half of his uniform off before he even realized which half she'd gone for.

That's when a notification chime sounded over the colony's intercom. "The emperor's honored guests may enter the paradise of the Gail Crater enclosure at will."

Sahra raised his undershirt and kissed down his bare chest on her way to parts unknown to a virtuous woman like her. He intercepted her, ripping open her uniform top to nuzzle her larger than the average Asian sized breasts as he reached around her back to unfasten her bra.

"Oh, how I wish I were there." The Matchmaker cooed gleefully. "I can't be sure what I'd choose, to watch this union or walk out into my utopian Eden." He cackled with laughter. "They didn't even make it to the apartment. The pills have left them no self-control whatsoever."

The camera crew zoomed in on Sahra's exquisitely formed breasts. Cody pulled her against his chest so they couldn't see, kissing her with reckless abandon as she stripped more clothing.

That's when Holden strode along the hallway dropping the guards and then the camera crew with a pair of laser pistols before he destroyed the transmitter. Sahra spit out the pink pill, reaching for her clothing. Cody struggled for breath on the tiled floor wearing nothing but his socks, a shoe, and his undershorts.

"Thank heaven you made it in time." Sahra dressed quickly.

"Happy to be of service, Ma'am." Holden nodded with a smile, then blew on the barrels of his guns, glancing at Cody. "I'm glad I didn't have to beat you off of her."

"Remind me to send a gift basket to Nurse Hasklin." Sahra smiled, fully clothed. "She is a fast fingered one, that's for sure."

"She palmed the pill, and that's when I knew something was happening." Cody dressed fast. "What's this about walking out into the crater?"

"The elites and their cronies are outside celebrating their last breaths." Holden pressed the button to order the elevator.

"What do you mean?" Cody felt as out of the loop of understanding as Lisa often seemed to.

"My crew could have survived out there for weeks now with only oxygen masks." Sahra entered the elevator with Holden. "Unfortunately, the Shim Bush bacteria only aerosolizes as the fruit ripens."

"And I suppose you just kept that piece of information to yourself?" Cody had never guessed that the Shims were capable of this level of cunning. "The crater was never going to be habitable, was it?"

"Not unless you've already had the fever and survived." She grabbed one of Holden's pistols. "Now, let's take the command center and free the slaves."

Cody grinned as he balled his fists, ready to topple a tyrannical government from the ground up.

Chapter Forty

Alone and grief stricken for hurting Royce, Lisa walked through the sand toward Shade's workshop. Pouring her heart out in prayer for Royce's safety and that of the crew, she rounded a curve in the canyon to find the sun rising at the end of a long passage. Stunned by the unparalleled beauty before her, she waked further in a state of awe.

The light increased until the deep red color of the sandstone lightened to shades of orange with streaks of almost white in places. Some of the stratified layers of rock had worn away while others remained. In the distance, a tree grew in the center of a wider section.

As she approached it, the leaves rustled so pleasantly that she couldn't help smiling. The gentle fragrance of citrus fruit grew stronger. And as she strode determinedly forward, she discovered that oranges dotted tree branches and waxy, emerald leaves glistened in the sunlight.

The smell of earth and the spray of a watering system gave her a sense of reality. However, it was the blue sky seen through the lens of glass above that made it feel as if this were Earth and not Mars. That combined with the heat in this canyon caused her to pick a piece of fruit to quench her thirst.

Royce had gone, pursuing a course of vengeance. Yet, thinking of it like that didn't feel right. Perhaps, it truly was justice that he sought.

Cody needed justice. Royce could give it to him. But as for her, she had only ever hoped to free the people of Mars through a different sort of revolution.

She had dreamed of reviving the planet's core and restoring the electromagnetic field of Mars. Evidence indicated that a field had once shielded the planet, holding the atmosphere safe from the solar winds that stripped it away without one. But something had changed, leaving the planet defenseless.

Lisa glanced around. A rusty door lay embedded in the rock face. It blended in, but someone had painted in green lettering the words 'Shade Tree Mechanic.'

This was Erica's workshop. The weight of the realization made her existence more concrete. Cody had loved her all his life.

If she hadn't killed her, then he would be with her right now. That would have left Lisa free to love Royce. Yet, that wasn't how it had turned out.

Lisa closed her eyes and tears slipped between her eyelashes. She loved Royce, but she loved Cody more, deeper, and in a way that left no room for anyone else to take his place. He didn't understand, and she grieved for having hurt him, but there was no help for it.

Lisa grasped the doorknob of Shade's workshop. The lock wouldn't budge. Letting out a slow breath, she pulled a hairpin and slid it through the side of the mechanism and then typed in the numbers one through five in ascending order.

Lisa's tried and true method of breaking into this type of lock failed. Had Shade corrected the vulnerability? Her level of respect for the woman raised yet again.

Using the alphanumeric keypad, Lisa tried Cody's name with the number eight. That's where she had guessed he was actually from since he'd admired the palm trees there with such fondness. The locking mechanism slowly opened.

Upon entering the cluttered mess of electrical components, junk, and workbenches at every angle, Lisa flipped on the electricity. No doubt Flaco would bill her for that. Direct sunlight streamed in a south facing wall of transparent aluminum windows complete with a large vehicle sized airlock to illuminate the red sandstone walls and dusty floor in the workshop.

Condensation caused water to drip on dandelions in planters along the base of the windows. Experiments and components cluttered the rectangular space except for in the living area. Baby clothes and toys lay in a playpen of sorts.

This was where Shade had lived and raised her son. Lisa walked to a planter box and plucked a leaf from a dandelion, chewing it for good health. The bitter herb was edible in its entirety, but she wasn't hungry enough for that to appeal to her anymore.

The sun hadn't yet warmed the room, so Lisa turned on a heater in the corner. A communications unit sat covered in dust on a workbench nearby. With the press of a button, radio signals crackled from the speakers.

Royce and the crew bantered back and forth with the revolutionaries as they loaded the assault vehicles with equipment, arms, and provisions. The crew, however, would travel to NINE's perimeter fence in the rover from Lisa's wreck last month. They'd have to wear suits since it didn't hold air, but repairing the broken wheel and recharging the life support systems had been relatively easy compared to what some of the other craft needed.

Lisa listened to their comforting chatter as she looked over the laboratory tables. Among the mechanical detritus, she discovered a clear plastic model of Earth and its moon. Spinning the satellite in its orbit, Lisa noticed a startling effect.

Tiny dark particles inside the liquid filled globe followed the moon. Struck by the simplicity of the concept, Lisa stared at it in fascination. A notebook lay open beside the model, and she read through the pages with increasing enthusiasm.

The model ran on the principles of simple magnetism. The moon held a magnet, and the globe held metal shavings in water. Yet, that's not the force described in the notebook.

Shade had speculated that it was the gravitational pull of the moon, causing tidal forces to move a completely molten planet core in the same way it pulled the oceans that created the electromagnetic field protecting Earth. Lisa had never heard this theory before, but it seemed logical on the surface. Yet, how could that help Mars?

Scientists had long believed that the planet had cooled, solidified in the center, and that was why the electromagnetic field had failed. Yet, Shade's notes refuted accepted science, postulating that the sporadic pockets of electromagnetism on Mars proved that the planet's core was still molten. She called them eddies and correlated them with the orbits of Phobos and Demos, Mars' two small moons.

Lisa considered the idea despite the lack of hard data or accurate calculations. Allowing her imagination to run wild, she collided with the fact that according to this thought experiment, the moons could never have created a field at all. Flipping ahead in the notebook, Shade theorized that Mars must have had one large moon in its ancient past.

Lisa sighed, bowing her head in prayer. Did Shade's musings have merit? Startlingly, the light and warmth of the Spirit of God illuminated the idea until it became a pathway forward.

Even if this wasn't right, the confirmation that it would lead Lisa to the solution that would revive the planet caused her to sob with joy. God had given Shade the answer. A slave in a dungeon had needed it more than Lisa did because it had given her hope in her darkest hours.

Dusting off her hands, Lisa took heart and set to work on a project that would probably take the rest of her life.

Chapter Forty-One

"Why are the lights on in my mother's high-rise offices?" Royce stared through the transparent aluminum dome of the promenade in NINE at the administrative tower built off from the ocean habitat.

"We've searched everywhere else. We might as well look there." Flaco ran a hand through his short cropped, regulation length, dark hair with a look of regret on his face.

"It'll grow back." Royce clapped a hand on his friend's shoulder.

"Sure." Flaco shook his head.

"At least it wasn't the world's most magnificent beard." Another crew member stroked his clean shaven chin with a sorrowful expression.

Royce chuckled. He'd never understand men and their hair obsessions. He counted himself lucky to have the little he did have.

The group had infiltrated NINE with exactly the same ease as Lisa had predicted. Wearing plain clothes and protected by the computer's security protocols, they had searched the entire colony without any problems. Everything here seemed to be running normally, but the Matchmaker had eluded detection.

"Follow me." Royce led the way.

The crew trailed him like a bunch of buddies out for a good time. Passing under the tall pine trees, they bantered back and forth in good-natured conversation. The sun shone low on the horizon and most of the crowds were clearing for the night.

Exiting the promenade, they made their way through a hallway to the administrative office building. In the lobby, they passed the empty receptionist's desk. Deeper into the building, they came to the office of the counselor's personal assistant and a private elevator.

"Tammy, I'd like to visit my mother's office, please." Royce pulled a stun pistol from under his jacket, pointing it at his mother's long-time secretary.

Tammy did a double-take, but smoothly recovered. "She isn't in at the moment, Mr. Greene, but I'm happy to send you up to join your grandfather and his eight guests. One of them is your friend, Director Tran. She'll be relieved to see you." Tammy pressed a button and the luxurious elevator door opened.

Royce and the crew entered the glass elevator car inside a cylindrical aquarium filled with tropical fish. His mother had a connection with the ocean because her husband had been an marine biologist. They ascended five stories to the sunny bubble shaped office of Gold Council Leader Addison Albright.

As the doors opened, they rushed into the elegant office with their pistols drawn. Stunning the six guards as fast as possible, they took blasts that dropped all but Royce and Flaco. That left the Matchmaker and Andrea Tran still conscious.

"Hello, Grandfather." Royce glared at the deathly pale deviant laying in a hospital bed hooked to a dozen machines with Doctor Tran handcuffed to his bedside.

"Who's there?" The old man's eyelids lifted slightly.

"I'm Addison Albright's son." Royce cautiously drew closer. "You remember your daughter, don't you?"

"Yes, but she isn't important anymore." He coughed, struggling for breath.

"Right." Royce stood up straight. "That's because you triggered the kill switch you had implanted in her brain. Now, she's not important to anyone, except the ones who loved her like me."

"The good Doctor Tran here, helped me with the design of that implant." The Matchmaker emitted a juicy sounding chuckle. "She seems to regret that, though, especially after I had one put in her head." He lifted his left hand to reveal a small device with a bright red button in the center. "Now, she has no choice but to obey my every whim."

"Andrea, are you all right?" Royce looked her over, finding bruising and her arm in a sling.

"Don't worry about me." She met his gaze with apparent resignation.

"Oh, but you should worry about her well-being." The Matchmaker raised his hand, poising his trembling thumb over the red button.

"Why?" Royce drew closer as Flaco stood his ground. "Are you going to kill her? I wouldn't advise it. She's all that stands between you and justice in a court of law."

"And who's going to testify against me?" The old man scoffed.

"I will." Royce took another step forward.

"You can't, you're not even human." The old man growled. "Who else is there? None left living."

"I'm as human as any man." Royce glared at the creature of his nightmares.

"No, Bone, you're nothing but a shadow of humanity." The Matchmaker rested his head on the pillow with lazy eyelids. "You're a soulless shell to be used for pleasure and discarded at will."

"I'm not soulless, Grandfather." Royce held onto what Lisa had told him.

"You are a sex toy and nothing more." The old man sighed. "But I must say that even as an infant, you pleased me more than your mother ever did."

"I know you molested her." Royce's trigger finger trembled with the effort required to prevent him from firing on the monster.

"I will admit to no such thing." He smiled weakly. "You have no evidence of any wrong doing."

"I'm the witness." Royce screamed, losing control as panic overtook him. "I'm the proof."

"You're a clone." The old man laughed darkly. "No one will listen to you."

"I'm a clone of your grandson, Cody Greene, and you're the one who created me for your illicit breeding program." Royce ground his teeth as Flaco turned his weapon on him.

"Oh, certainly not me." The Matchmaker smiled. "I'm just a lowly, Technology Division, computer programmer."

"You're the Matchmaker." Royce came around beside Andrea, passing her a small metal ring as he put the barrel of his stun pistol to the old man's head. "And the emperor of the Gold Circle."

"Clones are notorious for their delusional minds." The Matchmaker smiled at Flaco as he depressed his thumb on the red button.

Unfortunately for him, Andrea held Royce's mother's magnetic ring to the scar behind her ear, doubling over in pain at the disrupted circuit, but otherwise unharmed. Royce snatched the device from the elderly tyrant's hand, giving it to Andrea. Flaco pulled a set of handcuff keys from a guard's belt and freed her.

"I think that's enough video broadcasting for today, Emperor Albright." Tammy's voice sounded over the communication's equipment in the room.

"What?" The old man startled. "No. What have you done?"

"I've let everyone in the colonies know exactly what kind of child molesting murderer you really are." Tammy cut the connection and all the communications equipment went dark.

Flaco stunned the Matchmaker and clapped Royce on the shoulder. "Well, I always said there was something strange about you having so many kids. It's not natural."

"Thank you for not turning on me." Royce knew it was a tender mercy.

"Awe, well, us pirates have to stick together." Flaco chuckled.

"I'm deeply in both of your debt." Andrea bowed to Flaco and then met Royce's gaze. "Is Lisa all right?"

"Yes." He nodded. "She's safe and sound."

Chapter Forty-Two

Cody held the command center at Gail Crater for weeks as the revolution ended, the trials of the criminals took place, and the penalties under the law were administered. At that time, the New Martian Colonial Government held an election for public servants, inviting the people of the Northern Territories to reunify. Most of them did and their coming forward to swear the oath of allegiance was as televised as the rest of the process had been.

Lisa never came forward, but new of he discoveries traveled far and wide. Royce Nedge testified against the Matchmaker and performed the execution. The first session of the newly formed judicial court declared that clones were human with all the rights pertaining to that designation, though the ban on creating them remained in effect.

Once relieved of duty, Cody had radioed Royce and now sat on a couch in the man's scrapyard residence watching seven of his children run wild playing games while he cooked a delicious smelling dinner. Yet, Cody had no stomach for food. He'd come to bring Trina to her father and to see Lisa.

"Did you tell her I was coming?" Cody approached Royce after a day of waiting and some long conversations.

"No." He stirred a large wok of fried rice. "She enjoys visits from the children, but she seldom leaves her workshop now that I've returned."

"Do you mind if I go see her." Cody avoided Royce's gaze, unsure of where he stood.

"It isn't my place to keep you from her." Royce scowled at the rice in the wok. "She chose you. I wish it had been different, but that's how it is."

"But, I thought–" Cody ran a hand through his hair. "I was told you two were married."

"Yes and no." Royce shook his head. "She agreed to marry me out of compassion for the children. We never fully consummated the marriage."

"I have a similar story with Sahra." Cody's heart pounded in his chest half in panic and half in relief. "She and I provided a distraction for the Matchmaker while the elites and their entourages entered Gail Crater to die of the fever. I'm still embarrassed about how close we came to completing our union before Holden Martin, Andrea Tran's husband, rescued us from the guards and the camera crew. The marriage has been annulled now."

"So, neither of you had feelings for each other?" Royce served the meal to the children.

"No." Cody studied the man. "It was all for show."

"I didn't know that Sahra Shim was with the resistance." Royce turned off the heat under the wok. "There were so many secrets and lies."

"What aren't you telling me, Royce?" Cody's misgivings deepened.

"Emotions were involved with the intimacies Lisa and I shared." He clenched his jaw. "And I'm still in love with her."

"Everyone on the planet loves her, Royce." Devastated by the news, Cody squared his shoulders. "She's our best hope for a future outside the habitats. I'll talk to her honestly about my feelings and my shame. If she chooses your family over me, then I'll leave without an argument."

"There's something else, and I don't want it to come as a surprise." Royce left the food and the children to walk toward a rearward hatch.

"What?" Cody followed him.

"Did you watch all of the trials?" Royce glanced at Cody.

"Are you talking about Councilor Han's trial?" Cody had struggled with this revelation for weeks. "I know he faked Erica's death and held her captive in the dungeons torturing her at will for years."

"Did you know that she tried to rescue you on the night of your rover accident?" Royce balled his fists.

"No." All of the air rushed out of Cody's lungs. "The blonde woman crushed when Lisa righted the rover, that was her?"

"Yes." Royce cycled through the airlock with Cody. "I knew Erica by the name of Shade. And you need to know that she had a baby. She named him Cegory Eden."

Cody absorbed the information like a fist to the gut. Walking out into the canyon, he stared up at the heavens in torment. That's when the truth struck.

"He's another clone." Cody walked the sandy canyon with Royce. "And Lisa feels responsible to care for him."

"You know her well." Royce strode ahead and picked an armload of oranges. "I'll take these to the children and leave you two to talk things over in Shade's workshop."

"Thank you, Royce." Cody knew how hard it must be for Royce to walk away.

As Royce's silhouette receded into the setting sun, Cody faced the door. It read 'Shade Tree Mechanic.' And that's when all of the emotions he'd kept inside for so long poured from his heart in a wave of ugly tears.

He and Shade had received justice under the law, but Lisa's mercy was the only thing powerful enough to actually make anything right in this life. Yet, he couldn't ask it of her. She'd given so much to him and to everyone else already.

Kneeling beneath the tree, he faced east and bowed his head in prayer. Before he could enter that door, he needed to know that it was for her that he'd come. As much as he loved her and wanted to be with her, he came to a peaceful resolution that he would accept her decision gracefully.

Closing his prayer, he stood, crossed the sand, and entered a sacred place. Light shone in through the windows of the mechanic's bay sized airlock, though other lights illuminated the far corners of the large workshop. A baby slept in a playpen in a living quarters on his right.

Out in the mass of scrap metal and gadgets, an electrical hum gained intensity. A scale model of Mars with two orbiting moons spun in the center of the chaotic mess. Tiny lasers mounted on the planet's surface blasted a section of the model of Phobos. Tiny pulse beams from the surface pushed the rock pieces toward Demos in a dusty collision.

Lisa sneezed, shut down the experiment, and brushed off her blue lab coat with both hands. Tossing her eye protection on a workbench, she entered data into a large computer. Rolling her head from side to side, she rubbed her right shoulder as she finished.

Bracing both hands on the workbench, she bowed her head. With a sigh, she removed her lab coat and strode toward the windows. Flipping on traditional Korean music, she took up two sticks wrapped with pink cloth strips and stretched deeply before she started a graceful dance of swirling ribbons.

Beautiful as she was, her frown conveyed a tragic sadness that moved him. Baby Cegory stirred from his nap, scooting to the mesh side of the playpen to pull himself up on his hands as he watched her. Grasping the mesh, he tried to climb onto his knees and fell, issuing a cry that melted Cody's heart.

Lisa switched off the music on her way to the boy's aid. She gathered him up in her arms, soothing him with kisses and softly spoken words in Korean. Not for the first time, Cody wished he understood the language of her heart.

In that instant, she seemed to notice him for the first time. Her chest heaved with a series of rapid breaths. How did she know, even in the shadows of the entryway, that he wasn't Royce?

"Cody Greene." She breathed his name. "Thank God you've come."

Don't miss out!

Visit the website below and you can sign up to receive emails whenever S.V. Farnsworth publishes a new book. There's no charge and no obligation.

https://books2read.com/r/B-A-LKBI-TDNRC

BOOKS 2 READ

Connecting independent readers to independent writers.

Did you love *Tidal Pulse: Mars Revolution*? Then you should read *A Rare Connection: Inspirational Romantic Suspense*[1] by S.V. Farnsworth!

[2]

Flirty, French, heiress Nicole Moreau takes her hard-working, American best friend, Andrew Leavitt, for granted, until he puts his education at UCLA on hold to serve as a missionary in South Korea for the Church of Jesus Christ of Latter-day Saints.

She can't understand his devoition, can't seem to be happy without him, and can't stop herself from interupting his mission. Intending to propose, she botches the question and leaves heartbroken.

Andrew is deeply in love with her but doesn't react fast enough to prevent a tragedy.

---

1. https://books2read.com/u/bpElxz

2. https://books2read.com/u/bpElxz

Caught in the crosshairs of the private war between her French Intelligence agent mother and a deadly North Korean unit of kidnappers, Nicole becomes collateral damage.

Can her well-meaning grandmother give her a second chance to chose truth as well as love so she can heal from a #MeToo secret with the power to destoy her? Or will her mother's enemies exact the final revenge?

Read more at https://svfarnsworthauthor.com.

Also by S.V. Farnsworth

Fusion in a Fission World
Hard Start: Mars Intrigue
Tidal Pulse: Mars Revolution

Modutan Empire
Woman of the Stone
Monarch in the Flames

Standalone
A Rare Connection: Inspirational Romantic Suspense
Tucked Away in a Discolored Scrapbook: Creative Nonfiction with
Poetry

Watch for more at https://svfarnsworthauthor.com.

About the Author

Immersive Deep-Shelf Fiction

S.V. Farnsworth writes noble characters battling dark worlds.

She is a woman of international experience with a slice of life sense of humor and a love of nature.

The first on her father's side to graduate from high school, she overcame dyslexia to become a teacher at Crowder College in Neosho, Missouri. She uses the four languages she speaks to bless the lives of her English as a second language students and help them feel at home. Having lived in South Korea, she appreciates the gift of acceptance.

As the author of five books, she provides entertaining escapes into the human condition, providing the reader with a full range of emotions and a triumphant ending.

See for yourself at https://svfarnsworthauthor.com/books/

Read more at https://svfarnsworthauthor.com.

About the Publisher

Established in 2019, Stone Wolfe Press is an independent publisher that is pleased to have released both novels and nonfiction. Their published books include the following titles: *Woman of the Stone* (2019), *A Rare Connection: Inspirational Romantic Suspense* (2020), *Monarch in the Flames* (2020), *Hard Start: Mars Intrigue* (2021), and *Tucked Away in a Discolored Scrapbook: Creative Nonfiction with Poetry* (2022). The press strives to release two publications a year.